So Far Away

Everything Will Change
Book Two

P. O. Dixon

So Far Away

Everything Will Change **Book Two**

Image Used in Cover Art:
© Anna Yakimova | Dreamstime.com

ISBN-13: 978-1507545898
ISBN-10: 1507545894

To my beautiful daughter,
Elizabeth

Acknowledgments

I offer heartfelt thanks to Betty, Regina, and Ken: the former two for being such wonderful first readers and the latter for such helpful editorial support.

My deepest gratitude to Miss Jane Austen for her timeless classic, *Pride and Prejudice*. Weaving Miss Austen's words throughout my *what-if* stories is always fun. I hope readers, when coming across them, will smile fondly.

Table of Contents

Book Two

"Think only of the past as its
remembrance gives you pleasure."

Jane Austen

Home Again

In this, the first chapter of the next part of Elizabeth's life, it must be said that some things were just meant to be. Others simply were not. Were she asked if she had the power of turning back the hands of time, Elizabeth would be hard pressed to fashion a fitting response with certitude. Returning to the bosom of the Bennet family was meant to be a happy occasion. Pray she would soon realize what a blessing it was — for the Bennets as well as herself. However, it was hardly a blessing to have her whole world turned upside down. Frightening is what it was.

Would that she never knew what it was like to grow up surrounded by such a loving family. Then the separation might not hurt so much. Even if Avery, Lady Sophia, and she remained a part of one another's lives, things would never be the same.

The hardest part of it all was that she had no one she could speak with to sort out the confusing emotions without the risk of giving offense to someone or another. The one person who might understand a modicum of what she was suffering was far away in Derbyshire.

Tearing her eyes away from the carriage window, Elizabeth looked at her sister Jane. Catching each other's eyes, a happy smile spread over both young ladies' faces. Their reunion was a blessing indeed. What a joy it was to have her Jane back after all those years. From the time she learned of her true life, Elizabeth had endeavored to recall what she could of her early childhood. Glimpses of the times Jane and she had spent together as small children, though fleeting, sometimes made the briefest of returns over the past week.

Jane had been a true angel, as well as a source of prodigious information that Elizabeth duly needed to puzzle over in order to piece together what she was to expect of her new life. Then again, Jane would only provide the most flattering accounts of everything and everybody, and Elizabeth soon began to suspect her sister had a view of the world that did not completely meet with realistic sensibilities. Surely there was something of less than perfection in the world Elizabeth was set to embrace.

Elizabeth wondered about her parents, Mr. Thomas Bennet of Longbourn, and her mother, Mrs. Francine Bennet, whom she sometimes heard her aunt Mrs. Gardiner refer to as Fanny.

Fanny. What a whimsical name, Elizabeth considered upon first hearing it mentioned, which led her to suspect her mother, Mrs. Bennet, might be a bit fanciful, with hardly a care in the world about the sort of weighty concerns that often pressed upon her mother Lady Sophia.

She quietly sighed. *How am I to make sense of this newfound knowledge that I have not one but two mothers?* Elizabeth asked herself any number of such questions designed to give herself a modicum of assurance over what would be a rather unclear next few days, weeks, and months as she navigated the uncharted sea of uncertainty that stretched before her.

Elizabeth could hardly think about the future without her thoughts drifting once again to the past. Her mind balked at the notion of leaving everything behind. Everything she thought she knew about herself had changed, and this was only the beginning.

She stared longingly out the window.

"Pray what is the matter, my dear? You have grown rather quiet in the past ten minutes."

Elizabeth knew not what to say in the wake of her fluctuating emotions, and thus she remained silent. She reached out her hand in welcome of Mrs. Gardner's outstretched hand. Squeezing it, she gave her aunt a tentative smile.

Mrs. Gardiner said, "No doubt this is a great deal to comprehend and in such a short amount of time. I dare say there is no cause for unnecessary worry. Or are your thoughts in Derbyshire still, along with your heart?"

Elizabeth did not feel it was best to dwell on the matter of her heart at that moment. Saying good-bye to Mr. Darcy was far harder than she would have imagined it would be. With Avery and Lady Sophia, there was hope for a family reunion. However, in the absence of an engagement with Mr. Darcy, there was no telling when they might see each other again or even if they would see each other.

Would he wait for her? If yes, how long a wait might she consider reasonable?

How long is too long?

Then, too, there was the more weighty matter that had to do with his feelings about her true connections. Mr. Darcy had all but confessed that he did not particularly like the Bennets of Longbourn. That was but one of the reasons she had done all she could to hold at bay any proposal of marriage she suspected he was on the verge of making just before they parted at Pemberley.

How might I possibly accept a life with him when my future with my Bennet family is so uncertain?

As much as she had appreciated his comforting presence and his reassurance during those last days at Pemberley, Mr. Darcy's magnificent Derbyshire estate, she had to wonder if his sentiments would stand the test of what she was now embarking upon.

Her life was no longer defined by excellent breeding, untold wealth, status, and privilege by virtue of noble birth. The thing that had once bonded Elizabeth and Mr. Darcy – both their mothers being the daughters of peers – was no more. On the other hand, a future between them was not entirely out of the question in light of what she suspected would be her wholly reduced circumstances.

Though I am not truly the granddaughter of a peer, I am indeed a gentleman's daughter. This alone makes Mr. Darcy and me equals.

Elizabeth could not deny that Mr. Darcy's finding her Bennet family entirely objectionable when he met them last year might indeed prove insurmountable. She now knew enough of the story of how Mr. Darcy had come to Netherfield with his friend Mr. Charles Bingley at Michaelmas. During that time, he had been made aware of life-changing information, and he simply would not rest until he knew it all.

A subsequent meeting with her grandfather, Victor Montlake, the then Duke of Dunsmore, in an attempt to advise him of the fraud that had been perpetrated against the Montlake family, had ended badly. Thinking Mr. Darcy had met with her grandfather with ill intentions, the outcome of which had led to his untimely death, was enough for Elizabeth to distrust the former exceedingly and endeavor to keep him at arm's length. Even then, she could not say she disliked Mr. Darcy, but needing someone to blame for His Grace's death, she attributed it to Mr. Darcy.

How wretched she felt upon learning he had only meant to help her family, not harm them. Nevertheless, there was harm done. Her Montlake family was now torn apart. Elizabeth smoothed her black, bombazine gown. She still wore mourning attire, as she would continue to do for another few months. Indeed, it was but one of the reasons more of her things would not be sent to Longbourn — her new home. What use had she for fancy silk gowns and jewels?

A flurry of dizzying emotions was rampant in the Bennet household: unbridled enthusiasm, regret, recriminations, anxiety, grief, and elation. Ever since Mr. and Mrs. Bennet had received word from their brother Mr. Gardiner that their second born child was alive and had been raised by a noble family and lived the life of an heiress, they did not know what to make of their good fortune.

Mr. Bennet, at times, openly wept. His prayers had been answered. After all those years of wondering what it must be like to hold his little Lizzy in his arms, he needed to wonder no more.

Mrs. Bennet, having at times secretly blamed her brother, his wife, and even her husband for the loss of her second-born child, feared what the sight of Lizzy would do to the elderly man who had worn his suffering for his daughter on his sleeve like a badge of honor. Despite having four other daughters, he would not think of any of them as his favorite. There could be but one favorite, his little Lizzy.

Mr. Bennet, by now, was in a fair way of knowing Mr. Gardiner's letter by heart. Sitting alone in his library, watching and waiting for signs of an approaching carriage, he brushed his hand over his wispy beard. *To think, I owe my happy fortune all to Mr. Darcy.*

He threw a pensive glance about the room in recollection of the time the younger man and he had spent in that very room. Not for the first time, he wondered if Mr. Darcy had suspected a connection between the Montlakes and the Bennets even then.

I must find a way to thank Mr. Darcy for being the means of reuniting me with my daughter. I surmise the great man may be somewhat whimsical in his civilities, and he may very well find it impertinent for me to write to him, but it is the only decent thing to do. With such a purpose in mind, Mr. Bennet opened his desk, retrieved a piece of paper, and commenced doing that which he really did not like doing at all — composing a letter.

It was a rather confusing time for the younger daughters, who had simply accepted the fact that the second born daughter was little more than a cherished memory of their parents. The third eldest daughter, Mary, was a mere infant when Elizabeth vanished, and the two younger daughters, Kitty and Lydia, were not even born.

Now, their second eldest sister, Lizzy, was returning to the fold, and the greatest question in the young girls' minds was what would it mean for them? Specifically, what sacrifices were to be borne? Would Mary be expected to share her piano, and Kitty and Lydia their favorite beaus? Anxious thoughts were also accompanied by pleasing prospects. Surely their sister would be an accomplished young lady with a thorough knowledge of all the modern languages and an excellent reader with exquisite tastes and knowledge of all the latest London fashions. Mary could hardly wait to immerse herself in her sister's novels while visions of fine gowns and expensive jewels danced through the younger girls' heads. Surely their sister's wardrobe would suit the two of them just as well as it suited Lizzy.

As odd as it was, Elizabeth had a sense of being at home the instant she stepped down from the carriage. Sixteen years had passed and, during all those years, hardly a single day had gone by when she did not feel something was missing from her life. The question was how much of her true life had she missed? More importantly, how happy would her mother and father be to see her?

The receiving line that awaited her arrival was quite different from the long line of servants who greeted her upon every return after a long absence from the Dunsmore estate. This was in and of itself confirmation that she was a long way from her former life.

A young lady whose appearance was modest did not hesitate in stepping forward to greet Elizabeth. When the moment came to speak, she was, on the other hand, a bit lost for words.

Jane came to the younger woman's aid. "Lizzy, this is our sister Mary."

Elizabeth recalled Jane describing Mary as the third eldest daughter. She reached out her hand to her sister. "Mary, it is a pleasure to meet you. Our sister Jane has told me so much about you."

"I—I do not know what to say. I—I am so sorry for what happened to you." Mary then embraced her older sister. "I am delighted you are home — back where you truly belong."

Mary stepped away, thus giving Elizabeth full view of two younger girls standing side by side just a couple of feet away. Their manner struck Elizabeth as being particularly silly, and she supposed they must be Kitty and Lydia.

She recalled hearing how Kitty's appearance initially gave Mr. Darcy cause to suspect a family connection. Hence, Elizabeth's first inclination was to study both girls hoping to see in either of their faces her own resemblance. None was readily apparent, but then again, Elizabeth supposed, she did not spend nearly so much time admiring her appearance as Mr. Darcy did.

Jane introduced both girls to Elizabeth in their turn, which prompted them to bestow oh so proper curtsies, albeit combined with unrepressed giggles.

Next, Elizabeth's eyes fell upon the face of the woman whom she surmised was her mother. Elizabeth's outstretched hand was promptly ignored when the woman wrapped her arms around her daughter.

"Oh, my dearest Lizzy, this is a happy day indeed!" She placed both hands on either side of Elizabeth's face. "Let me have a look at you. Oh, I do declare you are as lovely as I ever imagined you would be."

Before Elizabeth could fashion a response, Mrs. Bennet took Elizabeth by the hand. "Come. Let me introduce you to your excellent father."

One look at the man who stood there told Elizabeth that mere words were insufficient for such an occasion as this. He seemed more nervous than she was. Her heart pounding against her chest, she raced into his welcoming embrace.

Comforted by his strong arms, it was as though time stood still. "Let me look at you," he said, loosening his hold and beholding her face. "Come now, my dearest Lizzy. There is no need for tears. You're home."

Her tears she could not help but shed. *Indeed, it feels good to be home again.*

A Great Tax

Elizabeth's sisters spent the better part of that first evening in her room. They were most eager to know everything there was to know about her and what they supposed was her fairytale life, replete with castles, elegant balls, and dashing gentlemen.

She was delighted with the prospect of getting to know each of them in their turn. For so many years, everything about her life informed her that there was something missing, despite the noble upbringing she enjoyed. She now knew the aching hole in her heart was there for a reason; she had been longing for her sisters, two of whom she never even knew.

Jane sat quietly by the fire, contented to let the other girls get better acquainted with Elizabeth. Occasionally, she and Elizabeth would glance across the room at each other, and when one caught the other's eyes, they exchanged knowing smiles.

Elizabeth's love for Jane was immeasurable. It was no wonder she had spent many of her nights dreaming of the fair-haired, blue-eyed, angelic creature named Jane. It was no wonder that, of all her dolls, the one she enjoyed playing with most as a child and the one she treasured the most even until this day was the golden-haired doll that she called Jane.

The next morning, Elizabeth got off to a later start than had been her habit owing to the household adjusting to its new routine. In addition to her companion, Miss Greene, Elizabeth's maid also accompanied her to Longbourn. She was not insensitive to the burden this must surely have put on Longbourn's existing staff. The subsequent knowledge that all her sisters shared but one maid was a bit unsettling to Elizabeth. If she knew anything at all about Avery, she knew he would have offered to compensate Mr. Bennet for the added expenses of accommodating the sister of a duke. On the other hand, her limited knowledge of Mr. Bennet told her that he would have refused such a gesture. No doubt her being at Longbourn would entail a great many sacrifices, as Elizabeth was beginning to find out.

When Elizabeth entered the breakfast parlor, Mrs. Bennet, upon seeing her attire, was utterly troubled. "Why are you wearing such a dreadful gown? Are you in mourning? But how can you be? No one in our family has died — at least not that I am aware of."

Jane said, "Mama, you will recall my writing to you that the former Duke of Dunsmore has recently passed away."

Mrs. Bennet placed her hand on her face in wonderment. "The Duke of Dunsmore? What has his passing to do with any of us?"

Elizabeth knew not why she found this pronouncement surprising. She had not been at Longbourn for a full twenty-four hours, and already she had discerned that her mama was prone to say whatever sprang to her mind without any consideration for how it might affect the sensibilities of those around her. Fancying herself nervous, Mrs. Bennet had the excuse of her need for contentment to temper anyone saying or doing anything that might arouse her vexations. In this matter, Elizabeth did not mean to repress her own desires. "His Grace is – rather he *was* – my my grandfather. You will give me leave to mourn his passing, I pray."

"Your *grandfather*, indeed," Mrs. Bennet spat. "You ought to know that I shall never refer to that monster as such."

"Mama!" cried Jane.

"Now, Jane, even you will agree that the man who was the means of tearing our world apart deserves no such approbation from any of us — not after what he did."

Everything that Elizabeth had come to know about her dearest Jane had taught her to know that Jane would not have told her mother about the duke's misdeeds. Jane's mortification at her mother's insensitivity confirmed as much. She could only suppose her mother had learned of the details through some other means — her uncle Mr. Gardiner perhaps. Elizabeth fretted over how this information had been spread throughout the local town of Meryton.

Would she read in her new neighbors' faces the questioning looks and the unmasked dismay that she would mourn the man who had stolen her away from her Bennet family when she was just four years old and raised her as his own flesh and blood for reasons of his own?

Would they question her sensibilities in honoring such a man? Would they, like Mrs. Bennet, regard him as a monster?

How she wished they would not — if not for her sake then for the sake of her Bennet family who surely would not want to be the object of any one's pity, and for her Montlake family, who surely did not deserve to be regarded as evil.

Elizabeth looked at her papa, hoping that he would say something — anything to let her know that he was not of the same mind as her mama. When he looked up from his paper and observed her doing so, he arose from his chair, tucked his paper neatly under his arm, and quit the room.

Such blatant disregard for her feelings was all too overwhelming and rather than sit there and pretend she had not been injured, Elizabeth raced from the dining parlor and headed up the stairs to her room.

Standing, Jane meant to go after her sister, but Mrs. Bennet halted her. Minutes later, Mrs. Bennet entered Elizabeth's room. She demanded to know what Elizabeth was about—why in heavens had she run off like that?

"What did you expect? I have spent the better part of my life loving His Grace as a granddaughter ought to love a grandfather. Such feelings do not fade easily."

"Surely you do not expect any of us to revere that monster. The man was a vile criminal who hid behind his noble status to get away with his crime for as long as he did. You, too, ought to see him as such."

Drawing a quick breath, Elizabeth said, "And what of Avery, the current duke, or Lady Sophia, the woman whom I have loved and revered as my mother? Am I expected to think meanly of her as well—to cast aside my love for her also?"

Tears trickled down Elizabeth's face. She looked at her mama — the woman standing before her who had suffered the manner of pain no parent ought to have undergone. Elizabeth felt as if her heart was on the verge of being torn to shreds. Reading in Mrs. Bennet's eyes what Elizabeth surmised was heartbreak; she placed her hand on the older woman's arm. "Believe me when I say I am exceedingly grateful to be reunited with you, with my sisters, and my papa. Please say anything but that you wish for me to choose. I cannot choose, nor do I ever wish to choose. Her ladyship has always been very good to me — everything a mother ought to be. I love her."

Mrs. Bennet placed her hand on Elizabeth's chin. "As well you should, my dearest Lizzy. I would never expect or want you to turn your back on her ladyship."

"Truly?" said Elizabeth, her mind a little more at ease because of her mama's comforting touch and her reassuring words.

"Indeed. I have been exactly where her ladyship finds herself. I have lost you before. There is nothing so forlorn as the loss of one's child. I would not wish such a fate upon anyone."

"Oh, Mama! Thank you!" said Elizabeth.

Removing her handkerchief from her sleeve, Mrs. Bennet commenced dabbing her daughter's tears. "There, there, my dear, all is well. Now, come along, young lady. Your aunt Mrs. Philips will soon be here as well as Lady Lucas and her daughters. I suspect Mrs. Long will arrive shortly after that. Why, all our neighbors are most anxious to meet you. Come along, my dear."

When Elizabeth and Mrs. Bennet arrived in the parlor, their first caller was already there. It was her aunt, Mrs. Agatha Philips. The younger girls' eager questions about the happenings in Meryton gave Elizabeth to know Mrs. Philips was a great favorite. Where Elizabeth had seen in her mother's brother, Mr. Gardiner, a sensible, sophisticated man, she could not say the same of her mother's sister. While Elizabeth, by now, suspected she was not alone in believing her mama to be a woman of uncertain temperament and little knowledge of the world, she only wished that were the situation for her aunt. Here was a woman who lacked everything of elegance and good graces if ever Elizabeth saw one.

Mrs. Philips's vulgarity was a great tax on Elizabeth's forbearance; and though the lady at first appeared too much in awe of Elizabeth to speak with alacrity, whenever she did speak she must be vulgar. The thought that Mr. Darcy may have spent any time in company with her aunt must surely have not bided well. Such a fate likely served as the basis for some of his disdain of her Hertfordshire relations. She had not been in her aunt's company for more than an hour before she began to consider that if Mr. Darcy never visited that part of the country again, she would be extremely disappointed, but she would in no way be surprised.

Elizabeth said a silent prayer of appreciation for her sensible relatives in town, Mr. and Mrs. Gardiner. Such pleasant thoughts gave way to another intriguing prospect: that being the heir of Longbourn whom the Bennets had yet to meet.

Surely our cousin Mr. Collins can be no worse than my aunt Mrs. Philips.

Not a Lady

In his heart, Darcy knew that Elizabeth needed to return to Longbourn to the bosom of her true family, the Bennets. He would have been lying if he said a part of him did not wish that Elizabeth would find the Bennets as objectionable as he did and that she would wish to have little to do with them in time.

Surely she will realize that her true place is with the Duke of Dunsmore, the only brother she has ever known, and with Lady Sophia, who is loving and caring. Indeed, everything a mother ought to be.

He had endeavored to avoid Elizabeth's questions about her family for fear that he would not be objective. How he disdained his friend Charles Bingley's youngest sister, Miss Caroline Bingley, for speaking so unguardedly about his abhorrence of the Bennets in front of Elizabeth.

Darcy covered his face with both hands. *There is no wonder Elizabeth would not allow me to speak the words that lay on the tip of my tongue that I wished to offer her my hand in marriage.*

They had agreed that what Elizabeth needed most was time to sort through the loss of her former life as well as embrace her new life, but what if, upon discovering her true self, she decided that her life as a Bennet was the life she desired? If the past had taught him anything, it had been not to take too much of anything for granted.

All promises of giving her time meant nothing in the wake of his desire to be with her. Thus, he arranged to travel to Hertfordshire and to stay there for the foreseeable future. His initial thought of writing to his friend Bingley to tell him of his plans was one Darcy promptly reconsidered. Surely Bingley would have been amenable to offering Darcy all the hospitality afforded by a stay at Netherfield Park, but that would also oblige Miss Bingley to preside at her brother's table. The last thing Darcy needed was to see Miss Caroline Bingley. He had rather suffer the inconveniences of a local Meryton inn.

The day Darcy was meant to depart, he received a surprise early morning visitor. He stood to greet his elegant cousin, Lady Victoria Fitzwilliam, when she waltzed into the room. After dispensing with all the usual civilities, Darcy said, "You should not have traveled all this way."

"I was worried about you. My brother Richard told me what unfolded here at Pemberley with Lady Elizabeth — but then again, she's not a lady, after all, is she?"

More annoyance than surprise graced his countenance. He had supposed when he was discussing the Montlakes' story with his cousin Colonel Richard Fitzwilliam that the latter would know without being told that it was a confidence not meant to be shared.

"She is every bit the lady she has always been."

"I suppose what I should have said is that she no longer bears the title — that she is nothing more than a country gentleman's daughter."

"My sister, Georgiana, is the daughter of a gentleman as well. What is the point of your assertion?"

"Well, dear Cousin, if we are to continue speaking of the woman, I suppose we ought to refer to her appropriately."

"Pardon my saying this, Victoria, but I have no wish to discuss Elizabeth with you at all. What has unfolded, by virtue of the truth coming out, changes nothing. And I would ask you not to take it upon yourself to inform others about the Montlakes' misfortunes."

"How long do you suppose it will be before all of society learns the truth? While this revelation has not dampened your esteem for her, it must surely be consequential for the rest of the world. The Montlakes will be scorned and ridiculed wherever they go."

"The duke is decent and upstanding. Society will not hold him accountable for what his grandfather did. The same may be said of Lady Sophia, his mother. They were as much victims of the late duke's duplicity as was Elizabeth."

"What you refer to as victims of His Grace's duplicity others may well regard as complacent perpetrators of his misdeeds. What a tangled web of deceit this is."

"What this is, Cousin, is none of your concern. I shall be very disappointed should I learn you have been the means of spreading gossip and innuendo about my friend Avery. Should I find out about it, I shall know how to act."

"Are you threatening me? I, who stood by you through all your long-suffering despair regarding *Lady* Elizabeth," said her ladyship, her voice laced with hurt and dismay.

While Darcy may have openly discussed his increasing regard for Elizabeth with his cousin initially, he ceased being so forthcoming when he began to suspect Victoria did not share his good opinion. "I have no wish to argue with you. You know better than most what Elizabeth means to me, which is the reason I will not suffer your snide remarks. Do I make myself clear?"

"Perfectly," she said rather unconvincingly.

It would have to do, for Darcy needed to attend to more urgent matters. "Capital. Now, if you will pardon me, I must be on my way if I am to keep to my travel schedule."

"When shall I expect to see you again?"

"That's not possible for me to say just yet." Indeed, he only knew he had to see Elizabeth and he would remain in Hertfordshire for as long as he needed to be there. "God willing, when next you and I meet, I will have won Elizabeth's acceptance of my offer of marriage."

Two weeks had passed. Truth be told, Elizabeth missed her home—her brother, her mother and, yes, even her grandfather. She missed her former life and manner of living. Not one night passed that she did not dream of those times gone by.

At first, she never allowed more than a couple days to pass without writing to Avery, but she began to consider that if his receiving her letters were the cause for such pain and heartbreak as she sometimes felt in receiving his letters, then she ought to write to him with less frequency. The same could be said of her letters to their mother. Elizabeth had long since given up on the pretense that she must not consider Lady Sophia her as mother. *I am blessed to have two mothers, and I shall not pretend otherwise.*

Avery Montlake, the Duke of Dunsmore, is my brother, and Lady Sophia Montlake is our mother. Not anyone who would dare to think otherwise is someone to whom I shall give consequence.

All this was easier said than done, for her Bennet family, when they would speak of the Montlakes, were far more likely to speak ill of them than to speak kindly. Elizabeth had learned to be tolerant of them, for she considered that was their way of expressing their pain. She would not allow that anyone who was unconnected to her by blood bore such rights.

Her brother Avery she loved more than anyone whom she was about to meet. He had done nothing but love and protect her throughout most of her life as a devoted big brother would. Lady Sophia was everything a mother ought to be, and though Elizabeth had been saddened by the revelation that her ladyship and she were not of the same blood, she rightly supposed that it took more than blood to fashion a family — much more.

She also missed Mr. Darcy. His being a single gentleman made it impossible that they might share correspondence, but she had hoped that his being one of her brother's closest friends would allow her to hear about him. Except Avery never mentioned Mr. Darcy in his letters, and Elizabeth began to consider whether her brother might bear ill will towards him for his role in reuniting her with the Bennet family.

She prayed that such was not the case, for, indeed, she owed Mr. Darcy a great deal of gratitude. Were it not for his persistence, the truth would never have come to light. As much as Elizabeth missed her former life, she was grateful for the chance to know her Bennet family. At last, a part of the puzzle was found. Her dreams of the beautiful blonde-haired girl with the angelic blue eyes had ceased, as did her dreams of the tall man with the tall black hat whose face she could never quite discern.

Chapter 4

Undisguised Curiosity

Elizabeth was no stranger to walking. Rather she enjoyed it, hence when her younger sisters prevailed upon her to walk with them to Meryton nearly every day, she gladly accepted their invitations. By now much of the novelty of being back with her Bennet family, where she belonged everyone always said, had worn off. No longer did she see wonderment, puzzlement, and undisguised curiosity in her neighbors' eyes when they looked at her.

Elizabeth and Jane often walked side by side in front while their younger sisters Kitty and Lydia skipped along behind them and their sister Mary lagged somewhat behind the party with her nose buried in a book.

Elizabeth could rightfully say that Mary was not at all like her sisters in beauty or in temperament. Perhaps that is why she had given herself airs of self-importance that bore themselves out as pedantic, even a bit conceited. Self-important is how she would describe the youngest sister, Lydia, as well, but for entirely different reasons. Lydia was wild and, perhaps by virtue of being the youngest and a favorite of her mother, thought far too highly of herself for a girl who lacked accomplishments.

Lydia's being out in society at so tender an age as fifteen bothered Elizabeth. The young girl lacked the sensibility of someone who understood what being out in society truly meant and Elizabeth reasoned that if no one bothered to check her, then she might be destined for more trouble than the Bennet family's reputation could bear. Moreover, by virtue of her sister Kitty's habit of going along with anything Lydia suggested, Elizabeth feared she might fare no better.

Jane was far too kind to think meanly of anyone and thus could not possibly consider all the perils awaiting girls as silly as the youngest two. Elizabeth's mind wandered from thoughts of Jane's sensibilities to those of her parents. *My mama does not possess the inclination to curb the younger girls' wild enthusiasm and my papa does not possess the determination.*

Elizabeth considered that this was yet another reason it was such a blessing that she was once again with her Bennet family – where she belonged – as she always reminded herself to say.

I shall be my younger sisters' keeper. I shall be the one to steer them clear of harm's way and be that shining example for them to follow.

By now, Elizabeth and her sisters were near the neighboring estate of Lucas Lodge, and they decided to call on the Lucases just in case the Lucas daughters might wish to accompany them to Meryton that fine morning. Elizabeth was especially fond of the eldest daughter, Miss Charlotte Lucas. At seven and twenty, she was practical, and Elizabeth found in Charlotte a sense of camaraderie she did not often see in her sisters, including her dearest Jane. With Charlotte, Elizabeth always fell readily into conversations that bore weight and consequence — much like those conversations she often had with Avery.

The coming days and weeks afforded many opportunities for company as Charlotte Lucas was from the neighboring estate. She and Elizabeth became intimate friends. Impatient to know how her new friend had perceived Mr. Darcy, Elizabeth's curiosity could no longer be contained. At length, she set up to resolve every particular with which she was concerned.

"No doubt, your family – indeed all of us – are indebted to Mr. Darcy for his part in connecting the pieces of your disappearance and reuniting you with your family, but you will understand what a shock it was to many of us that he would give himself the trouble," said Charlotte rather pointedly.

"Oh?"

"Indeed. The gentleman you know, and perhaps greatly esteem, hardly endeared himself at all to anyone when he visited with his friend last year. He was thought to be eaten up with pride, and he suffered a general disdain for anyone he perceived as his inferior."

"Perhaps what others perceived as his haughtiness was merely shyness. I know him well enough to know he finds it difficult to recommend himself to strangers."

"At the risk of giving offense, I would say it is more likely that he does not give himself the trouble."

Elizabeth had never been in the habit of engaging in any manner of discourse that painted Mr. Darcy in an adverse light. She was not about to start now. "For the sake of our growing intimacy, dear Charlotte, I would say you and I must agree to disagree. Mr. Darcy is one of my brother's—" here Elizabeth paused "—one of His Grace's closest friends, which afforded the opportunity for me to form a fond attachment to him as well."

"A fond attachment? Are you certain that is all it is?"

Elizabeth could easily surmise that her new friend was clever. This was but one thing that she found so endearing about the older woman. "The truth is, Charlotte, I do not dare categorize my sentiments in light of the manner of our parting in Derbyshire. You see, Mr. Darcy does not care for my Bennet relations, which must surely affect his regard for me as well."

Chapter 5

Sufficient Encouragement

Elizabeth saw Kitty and Lydia standing across the street speaking with members of the local militia that had recently encamped just outside of town. Their flirtatious manners and girlish giggles immediately drew her concern.

"There my younger sisters go again, making a spectacle of themselves," she said to Jane. "Let us go over at once and see what can be done to lessen the damage."

Elizabeth was caught completely off guard when one of the gentlemen, whose back was to her initially, turned and looked at her. He was just as surprised as she was by now.

It was George Wickham. *What is he doing in the militia, and what is he doing here in Meryton?*

For the first time since Elizabeth had learned about her true heritage, she had encountered someone who knew her and her past life. This was to be her test.

The tall, handsome gentleman bowed. "Lady Elizabeth Montlake. What a pleasant and wholly unexpected surprise this is seeing you here in Meryton. This is indeed a momentous occasion."

Elizabeth extended her hand, and he accepted it and bestowed a kiss. Seeing this did not meet with her sister Lydia's pleasure at all.

Lydia said, "La! Lizzy is no more of a lady than I am."

Jane's angelic eyes opened wide. "Lydia! Remember yourself."

"I speak no more than the truth. Tell him, Lizzy. Tell him that you are not the person everyone thought you were. Tell him who you truly are."

Jane placed her arms around her youngest sister's shoulders. "Lydia, this is neither the time nor the place." She proceeded to lead her sister away from the officers. "Pray you will excuse my sister and me, gentlemen. It was a pleasure seeing you, but I am afraid we must be off."

Lydia protested. "But I do not wish to be off. I want to remain here and speak with the officers, too."

Jane said, "And I am sure you will, Lydia, at another time. Pray do not make more of a scene than you already have."

When Jane, Lydia, and Kitty were gone, Elizabeth returned her attention to George Wickham, who, amid the confusion, was still holding her hand. Her gentle smile persuaded him that the thing to do would be to let go of her hand directly.

"Sir, I really must confess that there is some truth to what my sister Lydia said."

"Your sister? But how can that be? You are Lady Elizabeth Montlake, the granddaughter of the late Duke of Dunsmore." His tone took on a somber measure. "I heard of his passing some months ago when I was in London. Pray accept my condolences."

"You are very kind, sir. I am afraid that my story is a little complicated and certainly not something that I wish to discuss while standing here on the street. However, as Meryton is such a small town, you are bound to hear the story in due course. As you and I have always enjoyed an amiable acquaintance, perhaps you will do me the honor of accompanying me to that quaint little shop across the street for tea."

In truth, she and George Wickham were always cordial to each other, ever since their first meeting at Pemberley all those years ago when the elder Mr. Darcy passed away. It was her brother and

Mr. Darcy who had no use for George Wickham. Elizabeth could only suppose her brother's dislike of the gentleman was a consequence of his friend Mr. Darcy's fierce disapprobation. Elizabeth always considered herself a fair studier of people. Rather than choose sides in a matter that could have nothing to do with her, she preferred to form her own judgments.

Soon the two of them sat opposite each other. Elizabeth's companion, Miss Greene, sat off in the corner, thus allowing the two a modicum of privacy.

Elizabeth commenced explaining to Mr. Wickham the actual circumstances of her life — how the late duke's grief had compelled him to act as he did, how her own family had suffered her loss, and how they later rejoiced at being reunited with her when all reasonable hope was gone.

"So, you see that is the story of my life. All these years I could have no way of knowing it."

His handsome countenance colored with concern. "Now that you know, what is next for you? That is, if you do not mind my asking?"

"What is your meaning, sir?"

"Well, you mentioned that His Grace and his mother have assured you that this changes nothing as far as they are concerned. You will always be an important part of their family. I suppose what I am asking is will you remain here in Hertfordshire or do you plan on returning to the life you once enjoyed with the Montlakes?"

Elizabeth wondered if what the gentleman truly was asking was whether she intended to renounce her standing as an heiress. Then again, perhaps she was being a bit too sensitive. Her fortune, or lack thereof, did not factor into his question at all, and why should it? He had no fortune of his own to speak of, so surely he would not judge her or look upon her with disfavor.

Her silence encouraged him to say more. "Life has a way of defying our expectations. I was meant to have the living in Kympton when it became available."

Here Wickham paused but a second. "You will recall my telling you that the elder Mr. Darcy was my godfather?"

Elizabeth nodded in agreement and, thus, he continued his speech. "It was my godfather's dying wish, and though I did not always feel this way, it became my favorite wish as well. I was never meant to be a mere foot soldier. The living would have satisfied my every notion of what I ought to be doing with my life. Alas, Darcy did not agree and when the living became available he gave it to another."

Slightly taken aback, Elizabeth said, "I find it difficult to imagine that Mr. Darcy would have defied his own father's wishes if he did not suppose he had sufficient cause."

"Darcy is capable of far more egregious conduct. I better than anyone ought to know."

"Sir, if you will recall the last time we spoke, I mentioned that I am not in the habit of entertaining any manner of discussion that disparages Mr. Darcy."

"I suppose that makes him a fortunate man."

"I assure you, sir, I extend the same courtesy to you."

"I am pleased to hear you say that. Indeed it is a comfort to me to know that you and I have always enjoyed each other's company and we always shall."

Smiling, Elizabeth did not attempt to mask her pleasure that they were of the same mind. This was sufficient encouragement for the gentleman.

"May I see you back to your father's home?"

"Why, sir, I would be delighted."

Chapter 6

But a Dream

D arcy was lying in his bed, helpless to the world and barely conscious of what was happening to him. The last thing he recalled was making up his mind to travel to Hertfordshire to be near Elizabeth. His carriage had run into a terrible storm, and his driver advised him that it would be best to wait it out on the roadside just ahead. That was the last thing he remembered.

It turned out that the side of the road was not equal to the weight of the carriage. His driver should have known better, but he was a relatively new hire who was not so very experienced. The carriage tumbled down the hillside. Darcy was lucky to be alive.

In and out of states of laudanum-induced unconsciousness, he had a feeling of being cared for by his cousin Lady Victoria. It had to be her. He would recognize her scent, that of rose petals, from among a thousand women. No one wore the fragrance quite like her. If not for the fact that he had given his heart to Elizabeth, he supposed he might be in some danger from his cousin.

Being the mistress of Pemberley was all Lady Victoria wanted for as long as she could recall. She wanted it not for the prestige of being the mistress of such a grand estate, or for all the wealth and privilege it afforded. Being the daughter of an earl, she was already wealthy and she had a generous dowry of fifty thousand pounds. That alone was enough to help her attract the attention of the most eligible gentlemen from both near and far. She did not want just any gentleman.

For that matter, Lady Victoria did not even desire to be married to a peer. For as long as she could recall she was in love with her cousin Fitzwilliam Darcy. Oh, how she loved this man. It vexed her exceedingly that her obnoxious aunt, Lady Catherine de Bourgh, was bent on establishing the general expectation among family and friends that her daughter, Anne, and Darcy were to be married. Anne was not Lady Victoria's equal in beauty or in accomplishments, and yet Victoria's own family entertained the notion that Anne was destined to marry Darcy according to the favorite wish of Lady Catherine and her sister, Darcy's mother, the late Lady Anne Darcy.

How utterly ridiculous to think that Darcy would ever consider such a fragile, sickly waif of a person. Lady Victoria always laughed to herself whenever her family discussed the *would-be* alliance. She knew better, or at least she thought she did. She was so confident that she would one day be Darcy's wife that she did not even attempt to disabuse any one of her family members of the preposterous idea.

What was more, she and her cousin Darcy were as close as two cousins could be — that is, two cousins of the opposite sex. Darcy rarely looked at any other woman. Lady Victoria had even gotten him to make a deal with her that, should they both remain single on the third day of the third month of the year of his thirtieth year, then they would have no choice but to procure a special license and embark upon a union in holy matrimony that would put both of them out of their misery. Said misery was that of being two single people on the marriage market — he the target of every eager mamma in the *ton* with a single daughter and she the target of every single man in need of a wealthy wife. It was almost a game to the two of them.

This they often discussed in jest solely between themselves when they had nothing better to contemplate. *Of course, all that changed when he began to notice 'Lady' Elizabeth and her amazingly fine eyes,* Lady Victoria silently lamented.

Even though Darcy had set off to Hertford-shire, her ladyship had decided to remain at Pemberley for another day before returning to Mat-lock. Being the one who was at Pemberley when Darcy was carried inside on a stretcher, Lady Victoria had remained by his side ever since. With his sister residing at her establishment in London, Lady Victoria was effectively the mistress of Pemberley — managing things and attending to his affairs as though she were his wife while he gradually recuperated. During that time, she had many opportunities to appreciate nearly everything about the man who held her heart, including the most personal things that only a wife or a lover ought to know.

When they were alone, she would sit by his bedside and read to him. Soon, she began to notice what it meant when someone of the male persuasion was referred to as being a healthy young man.

On one particular evening, after she had dismissed Darcy's man for the night amid the dutiful valet's strong protest, she sat by her cousin's bedside. She could not help but discern his aroused state even though she knew he was sound asleep.

Her desire to pull back the covers and have a peep increasingly outweighed her concerns for what it would mean for their amiable accord should he ever find out. *What would be the harm?* She was curious after all. What better way was there to satisfy her curiosity than in the privacy of his bedroom where they were utterly and completely alone and no one ever need know?

Cognizant of what a scandal it would be if someone were to walk in and catch her gazing at her cousin in such a state, she crept over to the door and turned the lock. She then walked back to his bedside. Even her maidenly sensibilities were insufficient to quell her curiosity about this man whom she had been in love with for so long as she could recall.

She pulled back the covers and slowly lifted his nightshirt. What she saw was such that she dared not look away. She had seen marble statues and pictures in the gallery at Pemberley, in her family's home, and everywhere else where there were such prospects to behold, but nothing had prepared her for the sight she now feasted her eyes on — how beautiful.

Looking and seeing suddenly was not enough. She needed to touch him. At length, she commenced a lingering, trailing exploration that encouraged his ardor. She soon became entranced, which merely served to embolden her until the spell in which she found herself immersed gave way to a bit of reality when she heard him moan. She panicked. Jerking her hand away, she lowered his bedcovers. He did not awaken, which encouraged her to pick up where she left off, not only out of curiosity, but also for the fact that she was beginning to feel a pooling moisture — a moistness that she associated with him.

She drew the covers back once more. His ardor had not waned an inch. A thorough study of books that she should not have been reading had taught her that it was possible for a woman to engage in any manner of doings that required no participation at all from her partner. At such times as those, she even imagined what it would be like and when she did give over to such fantasies, there was only one man at the forefront of her mind.

Easing herself into bed next to him, she gave serious contemplation to doing those things to him that she recalled from the pictures. Her maidenly sensibilities aside, she longed for him. She needed to feel his hardness against her softness. Were he to awaken from his laudanum induced sleep and find her in his bed, she would convince him that he had been the instigator. She would be mistress of Pemberley in no time at all. Finally, she was on the cusp of having her fondest dreams come true. Lady Victoria was in heaven and she knew it.

Darcy's deepest slumber always promised the cessation of pain from his injuries, the riddance of tight bandages protecting his wounds, and the gratification of being once again with Elizabeth. This dream, while along the same vein of all the others of late, gave Darcy a sense of not being alone. But, of course, he was alone. He was merely dreaming ... Yes, dreaming of what it would be like when he and his lady love, Elizabeth, were united as man and wife. He often dreamed of her — of making love to her. Even though it was a dream he was determined it would last and last.

Amid the prospect of such intoxicatingly warm moistness, all he desired was to push and push into the utter blissfulness of the woman he loved, but he would not make her his, not fully. He would tease her there instead all with the intention of pleasing her.

A healthy young man, he not only wanted completion, he desperately needed it. How frustrating this dream was for Darcy, but he dared not awaken and find it all over.

She was beginning to move — to press her body against his with more ardent yet pleasing insistence. Was she ready? Was he ready? He and Elizabeth were not yet married, but what did it matter for this was but a dream — an intensely vivid and passionate dream, but a dream all the same. *What else can this be? Elizabeth is hundreds of miles away.*

It being a dream, he gave in to both their bodies' demands and commenced making her his. Her moans were intoxicating. What a cruel punishment it would be to awaken and not find Elizabeth by his side. *Savor this,* his dream state beckoned — *savor this.*

At length, he wanted to ease her from his body and slow things down, for he and Elizabeth had all night. Why was he unable to accomplish a small little thing like easing her away from his body? It was as if he were completely within her power. What a strange feeling for a man like him who was always arranging things for his own convenience.

She would not stay still, and with her lips pressed against his, he was powerless to beseech her to stop—to lie still. *Elizabeth and I are not yet married. We should not even be doing this.* Then again, it was just a dream. All too soon, he would awaken. What would be the harm in finding his release deep inside of her if it were just a dream?

It is but a dream.

The Most Deserving

The Bennet family would have been fools to fail to receive the young Duke of Dunsmore with the utmost deference inherent in his status. The Bennets were nobody's fools. Awe and wonder replaced hidden animosities upon his arrival. A true to life duke had come to call on them at Longbourn. Even the younger girls regarded him as though he were a handsome prince straight from the pages of an enchanted storybook.

Out of respect for the master of Longbourn, Avery's first order of business during his surprise visit was garnering a private audience with Mr. Bennet. He apologized for the pain rendered to the Bennet family. His grandfather's misdeed had been the means of a great scandal and there was no changing that fact. Nevertheless, as horrific as it had been for the Bennets, the same could not be said of himself. He told Mr. Bennet as much.

"Sir, pray you will understand that I mean no disrespect when I say that my life is richer because of my having Elizabeth as my sister. No manner of scandal will alter my great love for her. As I shall forever regard her as my only sister, any measures my grandfather undertook to guarantee her future happiness, I shall abide by. Please be assured that Elizabeth's dowry of fifty thousand pounds remains intact."

Having made no arrangements of his own for his daughters, whose prospects were severely diminished, Mr. Bennet was not of a mind to reject the young duke's benevolence. Having engaged in correspondence with the young man soon after Elizabeth's arrival at Longbourn, Mr. Bennet knew that the Duke of Dunsmore could be just as determined as Mr. Bennet was proud. The older man's pride did indeed balk at the notion of accepting any manner of charity that was the fruit of the late duke's coffers, but his lingering resentment would not be allowed to impede his better judgment. Elizabeth still considered these people her family. Hence, her dowry of fifty thousand pounds was her due.

A quarter hour later, when Avery and Mr.

Bennet had joined the others, Lt. George Wickham was soon shown into the room along with his friend, Mr. Denny. Elizabeth immediately bore witness to the disgusted turn in her brother's countenance. Knowing him as well as she did, his subsequent reaction came as no surprise to her.

Standing tall and proud, the aggrieved young duke said, "What is he doing here?"

Mrs. Bennet, concerned that her honored guest might be displeased, said, "Do you and the lieutenant know each other, Your Grace?"

George Wickham smiled and sauntered over to Avery with his hand outstretched. "Indeed, the duke and I are acquaintances of long standing."

Avery ignored Wickham's gesture. "On the contrary, this man is not an acquaintance of mine. Again, I ask what he is doing here, Elizabeth."

"Lt. Wickham is, of course, a guest, Your Grace, as are you, unless I am mistaken," she replied in a tone that only the sister of a duke would deign to use while speaking to him in the company of others who were so decidedly beneath him in consequence.

Changing his manner to be rather less severe, Avery said, "There is an excellent prospect that I saw on my way here that I should like to explore further. Join me, Elizabeth."

She knew that tone. Now was not the time to

afford him any opposition. "If that is your wish," she said deferentially.

"Indeed," said Avery.

Mrs. Bennet, again desiring to bestow upon him her most ardent approbation said, "I suppose you speak of Oakham Mount—it is a beautiful prospect indeed. Jane, perhaps you will wish to join your sister and His Grace." The fact that she intended Jane for the duke could not have escaped anyone's notice.

Avery said, "That is a very kind offer, Mrs. Bennet, and I should like very much to accommodate your request, but I need time alone with my sister — with Elizabeth."

Not long thereafter, the two walked along in silence for a while, one displeased and the other vexed. Elizabeth was the first to speak. "That was incredibly rude of you just then."

"Did you honestly expect me to remain in company with that vile man?"

"No doubt you are referring to Mr. Wickham. Why do you hate him so much?"

"I have my reasons. I take it he is part of the local militia. How long has he been here, and does he make it a habit of calling on you?"

"I fail to see what business any of this is of yours."

"So, is that how it is, little Sister?"

"Indeed, my dear big brother."

"I see you are as stubborn as ever. You ought to know that as I have been protecting you for as long as I can remember, I do not intend to stop now. Like it or not, you will always be my little sister."

"I dare say you will not have me behave any other way."

"No, I wouldn't. I never wish to see you changed. Now, as you are determined not to answer my questions in a manner that I deem acceptable, perhaps you and I shall discuss other, more important, matters."

Avery calling her sister and admonishing her, Elizabeth calling him brother and challenging him — it was as natural as night and day. Elizabeth dearly missed him. She laced her arm through his and rested her head on Avery's arm as they walked along, side by side. "This is truly wonderful. I like having my brother here with me."

"I don't know how long you will feel that way once you hear what I have to say."

"Pray you are not about to remind me of my duty to find a husband?"

"I shall never relinquish my responsibility to see that you are well settled, young lady."

"Well, it seems that you and Mama have a lot in common," said Elizabeth referring to Mrs. Bennet. With two women contending for her heart in that regard, in her mind she thought of one as Mama and the other as Mother. It was simpler that way.

Avery said, "A wise woman indeed."

"You may not agree when you find out her plans for you, Your Grace."

"Me?"

"You must have discerned that she has targeted you as a future son-in-law."

Avery chuckled. "Pray which of your lovely sisters does Mrs. Bennet have in mind as the next Duchess of Dunsmore?"

"I do not believe Mama cares which of my sisters you decide on as long as you choose one of them; though I suppose if left completely up to her, I think she would pick Jane, for she is the oldest and the most beautiful, and, if I do say so myself, Jane is the most deserving."

"I confess that I would be most fortunate to have her indeed. However, as you well know, my heart belongs to another."

Elizabeth chose to say nothing in response to Avery's pronouncement.

"You should also know that I have every intention of declaring myself to Miss Hamilton when the time is right."

While the duke was alive, he was determined that his only grandson would never marry Miss Margaret Hamilton owing to her low connections. Although her father was a gentleman, he had married a woman whose family's wealth was earned in trade. Heaven forbid that the future Duke of Dunsmore should tarnish the Montlake name in such a disgraceful manner by marrying so far beneath him. With the late duke's passing, Elizabeth could think of but one thing that must be preventing her brother from acting right away, that being the Montlake family scandal.

Avery immediately sought to change the subject. "You and I were discussing your future marital felicity, I believe. As I said, I shall not abdicate my responsibility even if I do have such a staunch ally in Mrs. Bennet."

Elizabeth knew exactly what Avery was about when he changed the subject. This suited her just fine. Miss Margaret Hamilton was the last person Elizabeth wished to discuss — ever. Elizabeth's spirits soon rose to playfulness, and she thought a bit of teasing was just what the occasion warranted. "Pray tell, dear Brother, do you have a specific gentleman in mind?" While her question was innocent enough on the surface, she was quite certain of the implications for both of them should he decide to be serious when she only meant to be light hearted.

"As it turns out, I do. However, I shall keep my opinion on the matter to myself for now, if you do not mind. Besides, there is a matter I wish to discuss with you. It has to do with Darcy."

Her pulse quickened. At last, she would finally be able to speak with Avery on a matter that was near and dear to her heart that she did not dare raise herself. "Mr. Darcy? Have you spoken to him? Is he in town?"

"I am afraid it has been some time since I last spoke to Darcy—not since we were all together at Pemberley. I did write to him, however; I have received no response that I am aware of. On the other hand, I have been traveling and should he have written to me, the letter may have gotten lost."

"I suppose there is the possibility that Mr. Darcy may have been traveling as well."

"If only that were the case, but I am afraid that may not be very likely."

"Whatever do you mean?" Elizabeth said, her voice heightened in concern.

"Elizabeth, there is something I have wanted to tell you, and I did not think it would be proper to write to you and tell you in a letter."

The tumult in Elizabeth's mind was now terribly great and all in a matter of seconds. Her heartbeat raced. "Avery, you must tell me at once."

"Darcy was in an accident. His carriage overturned."

Elizabeth missed a step and felt herself incapable of supporting her own weight. Avery gripped her by the arm in a tender offer of support.

"Fear not, Darcy is alive, but I understand he sustained extensive injuries, and for a time he was purportedly in and out of consciousness."

She sucked in her breath. "What type of injuries?"

"I know not the true extent of his injuries, but I—"

Elizabeth interrupted, "Oh, Avery, how could you have not told me about this sooner? I might have—"

"—You might have done what, Elizabeth? I understand that you and Darcy put all your differences aside when we were at Pemberley, but I am not aware that there is anything more meaningful between the two of you. Is there something that I ought to know?"

Elizabeth found herself unable to respond to her brother's inquiry. She had told no one, not even Jane, about the time she and Darcy spent together during her final moments at Pemberley, the words that were spoken, the loving and longing looks that were exchanged, and the unspoken promises that were made. But she could not pretend that she was not deeply troubled that he had been injured and that he might have needed her and not only did she know nothing about it, even if she had, she would have been powerless to do anything but sit and wonder and wait. *Would that I could get a letter to him, but how is such a thing to be accomplished?*

As pleased as Mrs. Bennet was to be entertaining the officers, for either of them might make a suitable husband for one of her younger girls, she was glad when they did take their leave. She was too much in the way of wishing for an alliance between her eldest daughter and the duke, and if she were to see her newest favorite wish come to be, then she needed to speak with Jane outside of the officers' company.

"Jane," Mrs. Bennet said, "I do wish you had accompanied your sister and the duke on their walk. You must seize every chance to put yourself in his path. It is not every day that a young woman is afforded such an advantage as you have. I am sure he would listen to Lizzy were she to recommend you to him."

"Mama, His Grace made it abundantly clear that it was Lizzy with whom he wished to speak."

"Oh, bother! He and Lizzy can talk anytime. No, you must do all you can to command his notice. As beautiful as you are, I just know you might be his duchess, but you have to try." Mrs. Bennet's voice took on a nostalgic air. "I was sure when my brother and sister Gardiner invited you to travel with them to Pemberley that it was at Mr. Darcy's request. I was sure he wanted to better his acquaintance with you, but nothing became of it."

Jane said, "On the contrary, Mama. Something wonderful came of it. I was reunited with my sister, and I owe it all to Mr. Darcy."

"Yes—yes, of course, there is that. But what I mean is there was no mention of any offer of marriage."

Disappointed, Jane said, "Is that all you think about?"

Her voice heightened, Mrs. Bennet cried, "Indeed, and when you do manage to secure a husband and proceed to have a house full of daughters, I wager it is all you will think about as well."

Mrs. Bennet grabbed her handkerchief and pressed it against her forehead. "I do declare that none of you have any compassion at all for my nerves." She stood and walked over to the window. Turning to face her daughter, she said, "First Mr. Bingley, then Mr. Darcy—two wealthy single men whom I allowed to get away. Well, I am determined that at least one of my girls shall marry the duke, and I shall not rest until it comes to be."

At that moment, her husband wandered into the room with a letter in his hand. "I hope that you have ordered a splendid dinner, my dear, because it seems we are to expect an addition to our family party."

"No doubt you are speaking of the duke. Why, of course, I have told cook to prepare a fine table."

"I am not speaking of the duke, but another guest with a distinction of his own."

Confusion glossed over Mrs. Bennet's eyes. "Someone more distinguished than the duke? Who could possibly be more illustrious than His Grace?"

"Why, it is the heir of Longbourn, my cousin, Mr. William Collins."

Having never even met the man, Mrs. Bennet was sure she never wanted the opportunity. "Oh, Mr. Bennet, say anything but that we are to receive that terrible man. You know I cannot bear the thought of him."

"I imagine it is hard to countenance such a prospect, my dear, for, as we all know, when I am dead, he may turn you all out of this house as soon as he pleases. However, he writes with the express purpose of rectifying what he avows is a wrong to our family."

He looked at his eldest daughter. "Jane, I'm glad you are here for it saves me the trouble of seeking you out. You must listen to what Mr. Collins has to say."

Mr. Bennet perused the missive for a moment or two, silently muttering to himself before speaking coherently. "Here it is. I dare say that you will be pleased as well, my dear Mrs. Bennet." He began reading aloud:

As a clergyman, moreover, I feel it my duty to promote and establish the blessing of peace in all families within the reach of my influence. On these grounds, I flatter myself that my present overtures are highly commendable and that the circumstance of my being next in the entail of Longbourn estate will be kindly overlooked on your side and not lead you to reject the offered olive branch. I cannot be otherwise than concerned at being the means of injuring your amiable daughters, and beg leave to apologize for it, as well as to assure you of my readiness to make them every possible amends — but of this hereafter.

Neither Mrs. Bennet nor her eldest daughter was very impressed by what they heard, which encouraged Mr. Bennet to be more forthcoming. "Do you not know what this means?"

"Other than your cousin appears to be somewhat of a rambling buffoon, I dare say that I have not the slightest notion of what he is saying."

"Mr. Collins means to choose a bride from

among our five daughters!" Preparing to leave the women to determine what they would of this happy news, Mr. Bennet said, "If Mr. Collins is disposed to make them any amends, I shall not be the person to discourage him, regardless of which one he chooses."

Chapter 8

A Much Better Man

Not wanting to give rise to the notion that he was above spending the evening at Longbourn with Elizabeth's Bennet relations, Avery sat around the fireplace with everyone and listened to Collins read from his book. At morning's first light, he planned to return to London. Nothing would have pleased him more than to bring Elizabeth back to their Grosvenor Square home where she belonged, but he suspected she would not be a willing party to such a scheme. Soon, he prayed, she would awaken to the fact that it took more than blood to fashion a family. Surely the latest addition to the Bennet family party would be confirmation enough in due time.

Elizabeth was certainly not inclined to leave her sister Jane at such a time as this. Mr. Collins's letter, having done away with much of her mother's ill-will towards him, made him a most honored guest. Rather than allow a single moment to pass without advancing her cause, Mrs. Bennet recommended Jane as the one that Mr. Collins ought to admire as soon as she learned the duke would be taking his leave of Hertfordshire.

Elizabeth was exceedingly vexed. Better that her mother had chosen Mary for Mr. Collins. She, at least, tolerated the man who proved himself to be quite ridiculous with his sycophantic manner. *Although, I really think Mary deserves a much better man as well.*

Kitty and Lydia found nothing about their cousin of interest to themselves. Perhaps had he come in a red coat he may have recommended himself. But, of course, his being the parson of his noble patroness Lady Catherine de Bourgh, as he frequently boasted, allowed for no such attire.

And although Jane likely found nothing in the man that would recommend his suit, her character did not allow her to speak of it. She suffered his attention with the patience of a saint and the smiles of an angel. That was what concerned Elizabeth most about Mrs. Bennet's scheme for Jane: the very real possibility that her eldest sister would concede to her mama's wishes.

Elizabeth had not been in company with Mr. Collins over a quarter hour before she suffered an undeniable dislike for the man. Making matters worse, she and her sisters were not the only objects of his admiration. He seemed to look upon the hall, the dining parlor, and all its furniture as his own future property.

How this business of Longbourn's entail frustrated Elizabeth and served as a reminder of her mother's and sisters' dire straits should a terrible fate suddenly befall her father. She was not at all insensitive to the fact that, despite her being a Bennet by blood, her family's fate truly was not her own. She had other choices, and it would be foolish of her to suppose otherwise. This was reason enough for her to reaffirm her commitment to raising her family's lot in life.

After dinner one evening, Elizabeth listened while her mama and Mr. Collins pontificated on the subject of his future marital felicity and how it must please his noble patroness. Mr. Collins was not a sensible man, which gave Elizabeth to wonder at his being Mr. Darcy's aunt's vicar.

What must it say for her that her parson is a mixture of pride, obsequiousness, and self-importance? Elizabeth could hardly wait to meet the grand lady and learn all about her.

Not wanting to engage in conversation with the gentleman directly, Elizabeth contented herself with listening in on his discourse with Mrs. Bennet.

"Indeed, my noble patroness, Lady Catherine de Bourgh, has been most generous in allowing me to be away for a se'ennight. She contends that is more than enough time for me to choose a wife. I cannot thank you enough for obliging me in this regard and recommending your eldest daughter, who is by far the loveliest creature my eyes have ever beheld." As if not wanting to give offense, he looked at Elizabeth. "Although, I should have been equally pleased with your second eldest, whom I dare say is your eldest daughter's equal in beauty."

"Oh, but my Jane *is* the eldest and, by virtue of her age and beauty, the most deserving. What is more, she has a temperament that must surely be pleasing to her ladyship," Mrs. Bennet insisted.

"Indeed. I am quite aware that the honor I am about to bestow is strictly Miss Bennet's due to her seniority."

Elizabeth, by now had heard enough of her mama's scheming and her cousin's contrivances. She went to sit next to Jane by the fire. The prospect that she would ever see her Jane settled with such a man was untenable. *Indeed, I shall never abide it.*

A few days had passed since Elizabeth had seen her friend Charlotte Lucas. The next morning, the ladies of Lucas Lodge called on the ladies of Longbourn, and when the visit was nearing an end, Elizabeth and Charlotte stole away from the others for a walk by the shrubbery.

Strolling along, arm in arm, Charlotte said, "I'm sorry that I did not have an opportunity to meet the duke when he was here owing to my ill health."

"I dare say you would have liked him very much," said Elizabeth, always supposing Avery to be well received wherever he went.

"My dear Eliza, he is a duke. What is there not to like?"

"He is indeed," Elizabeth replied, unable to discern if her new friend was merely teasing or perhaps a bit mercenary. She would hate to think it was the latter.

"Mr. Collins seems like a pleasant sort of gentleman."

"If you equate pleasantness with ridiculousness, I suppose you may have a point, my dear Charlotte."

"I do not suppose he is as bad as all that. After all, he does boast of some rather lofty connections."

"I would not find him nearly so intolerable if not for the fact that Mama is intent upon an alliance between him and Jane."

Charlotte said, "There is no reason to suppose that Jane will not be just as happy with Mr. Collins as she would be with any other man. And he is the heir of Longbourn."

"I want so much more for my sister. I am not unaware of the pressure one feels to honor the wishes of others when it comes to whom they should be married to. For years, it was the favorite wish of my grandfather – pardon, the late duke – that I was to be married to a man of his choosing. I know myself well enough to know that I would have been miserable had events unfolded as he had planned. Should Jane yield to Mama's wishes, I know she would be miserable. Jane deserves better. Indeed we all do."

"Mrs. Bennet is only doing what she must in promoting an alliance for her daughters. You ought to know this is not the first time she has exercised extraordinary measures to see her eldest daughter well matched."

"Oh, pray tell."

"Well, you know Mr. Darcy, no doubt, but do you also know his friend Mr. Charles Bingley?"

Elizabeth smiled in fond remembrance of the amiable young man. "Indeed, I do. I have met the gentleman on several occasions. In fact, Mr. Bingley was at Pemberley when Jane and I were reunited."

Charlotte said, "By the time the gentleman took his leave of Hertfordshire, there was the general expectation that he and Jane were to be married. Indeed, Mrs. Bennet had even boasted aloud of its being a most advantageous alliance."

"How awful for Jane," Elizabeth cried. "What was my mama thinking?"

"Mrs. Bennet could not be entirely to blame for thinking as she did. It was generally evident, whenever Mr. Bingley and Jane met, that he admired her. And while those who know Jane best could surmise that she was in a fair way to being very much in love, one who did not understand her disposition so well would have been unlikely to discern her increasing regard."

"Jane is shy and, from what I can tell, does not easily share her true feelings with anyone," Elizabeth said in her sister's defense.

"That is true. However, if a woman conceals her affection with the same skill from the object of it, she may lose the opportunity of fixing him. What a poor consolation it would then be to believe the world equally in the dark."

"From what Jane told me of her history with the gentleman, she had known him only a fortnight before his leave-taking. Perhaps had the two of them enjoyed more time in company he would have better understood her character, and he would not have been so easily persuaded by others to abandon her, as I strongly suspect was the case."

"Oh, Eliza, there are so few of us who have the heart to be really in love without proper encouragement. Mr. Bingley liked your sister. I contend that no amount of coercion from anyone would have persuaded him to leave if she had done more to help him on, which brings me back to my original contention about your mother's current matchmaking scheme."

"Are you suggesting that Jane should pretend to have feelings for Mr. Collins that she does not have merely for the sake of securing an alliance? What of love? What of my sister's happiness?"

Charlotte was nothing if not practical. She said, "Jane's disposition would scarcely allow her to do anything other than esteem her husband. Where there is esteem, there is respect, which can be a strong basis for love. The happiness in marriage that you speak of, I have always contended, is entirely a matter of chance."

Misplaced Jealousy

Meanwhile, in Derbyshire, Lady Victoria knew that once her cousin was fully recovered from the carriage accident, he would make plans to return to Hertfordshire to be near that other woman. Even in his sleep, he called out that woman's name, which vexed her ladyship exceedingly.

Along with his recovery came his adamant refusal to be given any more laudanum, citing his desire to be fully in command of all his faculties.

Having taken to opening his letters, her ladyship had come across one from his friend Charles

Bingley telling Darcy of his plans to return to Hertfordshire and extending the invitation for Darcy to be his guest as soon as his health allowed for travel. She did not know how, but she knew she had to put a stop to this. After spending more than one night in his room, even if he had given no indication of having been aware of it, she was determined as ever that he was hers and she was his and that no one would come between them.

The idea of writing a letter and placing it in one that had arrived from the Duke of Dunsmore – a letter signed by *Lady* Elizabeth or whatever she was calling herself now that the truth was out – came to mind one morning. She knew in an instant how to act.

A horrified look graced Darcy's countenance when Lady Victoria swept into the room after a light scratch at the door. His man had fully attended him moments earlier, so at least he was properly attired. Darcy said, "Pardon me, but I am sure your being in my room breaks every rule of proper decorum."

She merely huffed, "Cousin, you speak as if you have something I have never seen before."

Darcy said, "It has been a long time since you and I played as children, and you were more of a tomboy than a proper young woman."

"If you insist."

"What does that mean?"

"Do you not remember anything that happened during the past weeks? Who do you think it was attending you so diligently every day?"

A disturbing thought flashed through his mind — one he quickly dismissed. "I am exceedingly grateful that you were here with me over the past weeks, but that does not give you leave to be alone with me in my suite. Just imagine what your father would say."

Darcy walked over to his dressing table and picked up his pocket watch. "I suppose you will be returning to Matlock soon, for I am ready to resume my travel to Hertfordshire."

Lady Victoria bit her lower lip.

Darcy observed her through his mirror. Turning to look at her, he said, "I know that look. You are hiding something from me."

"Pray you will forgive me, Cousin, but I took it upon myself to open some of your letters while you were indisposed. I even read some of them to you. Of course, you do not remember my doing so. A letter came from your friend Avery Montlake and inside he included a note from his sister."

Darcy's countenance changed abruptly. "Elizabeth? Did — did you read her note as well?"

"No! It is wholly inappropriate for a single woman to write a letter to a single gentleman to whom she is not engaged. I know you well enough to know that if you two were indeed engaged, then you would have told me. Thus, I could only suppose that whatever she wanted to say must be terribly personal; otherwise, why break with proper decorum?"

"You did say that the note was enclosed inside of Avery's, did you not? Surely he would not be a party to anything as scandalous as you propose."

Lady Victoria merely shrugged.

Darcy said, "Do not keep me in suspense. This letter that you speak of — where is it?"

"Do you mean the letter from the duke or the letter from his sister?"

Growing rather exasperated, Darcy said, "I am sure you know that I am referring to the letter from his sister."

"Yes, of course. Here it is." Retrieving the letter from her pocket, she walked over to where he stood and held it up.

Darcy outstretched his hand to accept the reluctantly proffered missive. "How long have you been carrying this around in your pocket?"

"I retrieved it from your study this morning when I learned you were awake and already making arrangements to travel to Hertfordshire. I do wish you would reconsider. You might suffer a relapse. You've only started to move around."

"I shall continue to recuperate during the long journey. Now, may I request a moment of privacy?"

"As you wish. Please, do not take your leave of Pemberley without first saying goodbye to me — promise me that."

Darcy looked at his cousin with concern. "You know I would never leave without saying goodbye. Why would you even suggest it?"

"I suppose that the prospect of seeing *Lady* Elizabeth would make you completely forget a great many things."

"Please do not start that again."

"Please do not start what again?"

"The misplaced jealousy — what else? I may not recall much of what happened before my accident, but I do remember your not wanting me to travel to Hertfordshire."

"I did not feel it was the proper time and that is all. However, do not let me delay you a moment longer. You must read what your *lady love* has to say. I shall await your presence in the breakfast parlor."

Lady Victoria reluctantly quit the room. Symptoms of remorse began to creep across her face. *Will he ever forgive me, should he find out what I have done?* As was always the case when she thought about him too long, regret was soon replaced by yearning as the remembrance of what she had done sent her not in the direction of the grand marble staircase to await her cousin downstairs in the breakfast parlor, but straight to her apartment so that she might satisfy her secret desire. She entered the room, locked the door, and threw herself down on the bed. Doing what she must, she made short work finding such pleasures as she imagined only her cousin capable of bestowing.

Now lying there, thoughts of her last night in his bed stole into her mind once more. It had become a well-rehearsed routine: dismissing his valet, locking the door, and climbing into bed next to him.

She still did not know whether he actually called out her name that one time or whether she simply imagined it. She would just die should his desire for another woman prevent her from realizing her fondest wish to spend the rest of her days and nights with him. Victoria silently prayed that soon any notion of another woman would be banished from his thoughts forever. Soon she would be his wife, and nothing would ever separate them.

When Darcy read the letter, he thought the whole thing very odd. Indeed. It had nothing to do with the style of writing or the tone of the sentiments so precisely professed, but rather the distinct fragrance of rose petals that emanated from the parchment. Was it merely a consequence of her handing him the letter? Had she read the letter, or worse, had she penned it herself? *Victoria, what have you done?*

Darcy could not believe Elizabeth had written those words. He would not believe it. This had to be a mistake. By the time he arrived in the breakfast parlor, he was surprised to see his cousin there.

Lady Victoria said, "Cousin, whatever is the matter? You look as though you have received unpleasant news."

Darcy took his place at the table and picked up the paper while the servant filled his cup with piping hot coffee. Once the servant was done, Darcy raised the cup to his lips and took a sip.

Lady Victoria said, "Did you not hear a word I said?"

"Indeed, I heard you."

"Pray what does *Lady* Elizabeth have to say in her letter?"

"You handed it to me; I am sure you already know."

"On the contrary, Cousin. As I said, I did not read your missive. Now, do not keep me in suspense."

"The letter states her desire to have nothing at all to do with her past."

"Does this mean that you have changed your plans — that you will not be traveling to Hertfordshire, after all?"

"That letter does not alter anything. In fact, the more I think about it, the more I am convinced that the letter was not written by Elizabeth at all."

"Are you suggesting His Grace wrote the letter as a means of keeping you from seeing her? Or his mother, perhaps? You once said the late duke did not wish for an alliance between you and his granddaughter. Perhaps Avery and his mother mean to honor his wishes."

Darcy looked at his cousin in silent inquisition. *Do I even know you?* "No, your ladyship, I am not saying that at all."

"Then what are you saying?"

"I'm saying my plans have not changed. I shall travel to Hertfordshire." Her ladyship did not even try to hide her disappointment. "I am sorry this does not meet with your approval, but what did you expect? Surely you must know that I am in love with her."

Her ladyship stood. "And what if she is not in love with you?"

Darcy stood as well. "Then that would be my concern, would it not? I have instructed your maid to start preparing your things for your departure to Matlock. Your carriage awaits you."

"Is this all the gratitude that I am to receive for being here by your side all these weeks — immediate banishment from your home?"

"On the contrary — you ought to consider this your recompense for attempting to deceive me."

"Of what are you accusing me?"

"I am recovering from a carriage accident that left me badly battered and bruised, but I am not blind as I would have to be in order to fail to detect your own handwriting even when cleverly disguised."

"You are in no state to travel. I am only looking out for your best interest."

"You went too far!"

Lady Victoria started to cry, leaving Darcy unable to do anything other than comfort her.

"Why are you doing this? You have known for months how I feel about Elizabeth."

Lady Victoria looked into his eyes and she placed her hands on his chest. "Do you not know how I feel about *you*?"

Darcy said, "You and I have always been close and while it is true that I love you, as I always will, I do not love you in the manner in which you obviously now wish. I do not know how to make myself any clearer, other than to refuse to see you again—to avoid you altogether," he said, taking both her hands in his and removing them from his chest.

With both her hands in his in that way, he had a strange sense that they had shared intimacies that they ought not to have shared. He released her hands as though they burned like hot coals. "This time apart will do us both a world of good."

"You're angry at me and it breaks my heart. Please, if you must go away, then you must. However, let us not part in anger. No one is more important to me than you."

"This is how it must be. I have written to your father and mother, thanking them for allowing you to be here and telling them to expect your imminent arrival at Matlock. Goodbye, Victoria."

With that, Darcy quit the room, pretending he did not leave one very broken hearted cousin behind.

Darcy's plans had called for his remaining at Pemberley long enough to see his cousin off. He was in his study with his steward discussing his plans for conducting business from Hertfordshire when a frantic footman rushed in and announced a fire was raging out of control. One of the tenant's homes had burned to the ground and several others were threatened.

Darcy bolted from his seat. "Gather all the men from the household and the stables. We'll need every able bodied man at Pemberley if we are to contain the damage."

His steward held up his hand. "Sir, no doubt you want to aid in combating the fire, but you risk further injuring yourself. Perhaps you ought not — "

" — Nonsense, man! It is my solemn obligation to stand side by side with all the other men to combat this fire." His concern for his tenants was brushed aside momentarily as his thoughts wandered to Hertfordshire and to the woman who was so far away.

Will I ever make it to Elizabeth's side?

His Own Deficits

As the days went by, much of Elizabeth's pleasure in the reunion with family was gradually replaced with shame on every occasion that found her sisters and her in public. More and more, she felt Mr. Darcy's objections were justified and entirely reasonable. She recalled the exact words he had spoken when she pressed him to tell her about her Bennet relations.

"The fact is that I found the Bennets wholly lacking in terms of decorum and good taste. Mrs. Bennet is a woman of mean understanding, little information, and uncertain temper. Mr. Bennet comes across as being so odd a mixture

of sarcastic humor, reserve, and caprice as to render him wholly detached from the rest of his family, and the daughters are silly, wild, and uncouth."

Finding herself in the position of agreeing with him felt rather treasonous, but the facts did not lie. Unlike Mr. Darcy, however, Elizabeth was in the ideal position to redress the rather bleak assessment.

Anything that gave her reason to think of Darcy also served as a reminder of how much she missed him. She had suffered many months apart from him over the course of their friendship, but none of those occasions had ever been accompanied by such loneliness and the aching uncertainty of whether she would ever see him again.

Thoughts of being in his arms, the soft brush of his lips against hers and along her neckline, could not help but intrude upon her quiet moments. When they did, she quickly pushed them aside. She had done the right thing in choosing a life with her Bennet family in Hertfordshire over a life with him in Derbyshire — in fact, she had done the only thing she could do.

Still, she missed him more and more each day and not knowing how he was faring after his near fatal carriage accident only made matters worse. Fortunately, there was the steadfast Mr. Wickham with whom she enjoyed spending time — someone from her former life whom she always found particularly diverting. So long as their discourse did not lend itself towards any disparagement of Mr. Darcy, Elizabeth enjoyed the lieutenant's company exceedingly.

The militia being encamped just outside of Meryton afforded frequent opportunities for balls and other social gatherings. The fact that her younger sisters were out in society before Jane was even married became an even greater concern for Elizabeth. It would have been one thing if the younger girls were well-mannered and comported themselves with proper decorum. But far from it, for it seemed no matter where they went they were determined to make the Bennet family look ridiculous.

Why her father refused to do anything to rein in her younger sisters, Elizabeth could not discern, but she was not satisfied to leave it that way. *Someone ought to speak with him and it might as well be me.* Having received every advantage in life desired by mortal human, Elizabeth surmised it was not her place to look down on her family when her presence might very well be the means of lifting them all up. Thus resolved, she knocked on the door of the library and waited until her papa invited her inside.

It had not taken her very long upon her arrival at Longbourn to discern that he tended to spend a great deal of time cloistered in that particular room. What was more; rarely did anyone in the house bother to interrupt him there, save her mama when she was in one of her agitated states.

"Lizzy, my dear," Mr. Bennet said when she stepped inside the room. "To what do I owe the pleasure of this visit?"

"Papa, I do not mean to speak out of turn," she began.

"I do not like the sound of that, for in my experience seldom does one commence a sentence with an apology and any good result."

"I cannot say that you are wrong, but in this case I fear what I have to say can no longer be put off. It has to do with the fact of my youngest sisters being out in society. I must admit to being quite shocked."

"Indeed, Kitty and Lydia have been out in society for years. I do not know that there's anything to do about it now."

"Well, certainly it is not possible to turn back the hands of time. However, it is certainly not too late for more judicious parental supervision and advisement. Who better than their father to teach the younger girls that their present pursuits are not to be the business of their lives? Lydia is not even sixteen and yet she is a determined flirt, and she is in no position to ward off any portion of that universal contempt which her rage for adoration must surely incite. And what of Kitty? She blindly follows Lydia wherever she leads. Papa, as they grow older and meet with larger society in general, do you not suppose that they will be censured and despised wherever they are known?"

"You make a good point, daughter, but if I may call attention to the obvious."

"Please do —" she hesitated but a moment " — Papa." After years of mourning the loss of a man whom she had placed upon a pedestal despite never having even met him and thinking of this iconic legend as her father, it was taking a while for Elizabeth to learn to embrace the fact that everything she thought she knew was merely a confluence of lies. The world-weary man who stood before her was her father.

"At the risk of offending you by pointing out the obvious," Mr. Bennet began, giving Elizabeth cause to doubt he took umbrage at offending anyone.

He continued, "Notwithstanding the despicable means of its coming about, the disparity between you and your sisters is great. Your dowry of fifty thousand pounds guarantees that nothing that your other sisters will say or do will diminish your prospects one bit."

"At the risk of giving offense," said Elizabeth in return, "I fail to see how your pointing this out negates my desire not to see them being mocked and laughed at by others and especially their father."

"My dear child, you are far too serious; a consequence of your aristocratic upbringing, no doubt. I always supposed that the very rich take themselves far too seriously and now you, my own daughter, prove it. You must endeavor to embrace my philosophy in such cases as this; for what do we live for but to make sport for our neighbors, and laugh at them in our turn?"

"If it is all the same to you, Papa, I would rather not make sport for anyone, least of all my own family."

"Have it your way, my child, but I insist that you will allow the same for me. I know your intentions are good, but there is only so much a man of my age can change."

"I contend that age is the perfect antidote for inadequacy in a father."

Mr. Bennet's astonishment was apparent. "Who is to say what manner of father I might have been? The man whom you so lovingly regard as your grandfather robbed me of my best chance and, in so doing, altered the choice of my life. For that I shall never forgive him!"

His hurtful words struck her forcefully. Yes, the late duke had injured her father as well as the rest of the Bennet family to varying degrees. Was this indeed a legitimate justification for his own deficits?

Mr. Bennet's constant reminding her of the late duke's failings was not enough to silence Elizabeth completely on the subject. "In time, you will no longer be able to hide behind the pain of what befell our family all those years ago. Then what will be your excuse? What then will be your reason for the neglect and general lack of regard for your family?

"You have a wife, whom you may perceive as dim-witted, but you chose her and if you chose her merely for the beauty she once possessed then shame on you. And while it is true she never gave you a male heir, she gave you daughters, daughters who need their father to guide and protect them — not laugh at them and deride them as the silliest girls in all of England."

"Now wait just one minute, *your ladyship*," said he, nearly spitting the appellation, "I will not have you stand there and render judgment against me."

Not wanting to continue arguing with a father who professed his love for her and yet did a poor job of hiding his distaste for anyone who dared to speak the truth, Elizabeth went away, satisfied with the knowledge that she had said what she came to say. Whether or not he chose to listen was beyond her power.

Now alone in her room, sitting at her desk, she opened her drawer and took out her miniature of the late duke. *Papa hates His Grace. Am I meant to hate him as well?*

After months of living with the people who had been harmed by him the most and even having some idea of the aftermath of what he had done to all of them – her papa's apathy, her mama's nervousness and Jane's shyness – Elizabeth still could not bring herself to bear any lasting ill-will towards the late duke. *At least not to the extent that those around me expect*, she considered. She had seen too much of goodness in him to allow even now that he might have been less than she thought him to be when he lived.

Elizabeth threw a reflective glance over the whole of the past few months. How far she had come from where she thought she would be at this point in her life ... the granddaughter of a powerful well-respected peer, which surely counted for something.

All that was not to imply that the late duke was perfect. *He was, at times, haughty, officious, and outright dictatorial – indeed the sort of man who liked to have his own way.* Were she to be truthful, she would confess to thinking herself rather blessed that she had escaped being married to the young man whom His Grace had chosen for her, but then that would be entirely too selfish on her part. *The man had died after all.*

She frowned. *Why am I dwelling on those aspects of the past when the remembrance gives me no pleasure at all, when really there is so much of both gladness and triumph for me to ponder?*

What was done was done and, despite the years of torment, sadness, and pain that her Bennet family had endured having had their child stolen away from them, now was a time for healing, for reconciliation, for forgiving. As much as Elizabeth loved knowing that she had a whole other family, she also loved the family she already had. Nothing would change that, ever.

Chapter 11

However Unwittingly

Awash in anxiety, Elizabeth paced the floor. When she was not pacing, she was sitting in the window seat. Sitting, staring, and waiting for a carriage that would not come.

Unwelcome thoughts flooded her mind on what could possibly be keeping Longbourn's imminent guest who was supposed to have arrived much earlier that morning. Her concerns were made worse by the prospect of what might happen when the guest did come. This was no ordinary guest. This was Lady Sophia Montlake. Mrs. Bennet, upon learning that her ladyship would be visiting Elizabeth on her way to town, had insisted that Elizabeth write to her ladyship at once to extend the hospitality of Longbourn.

Lady Sophia did not bear the silliness of others with a high degree of tolerance, and Elizabeth had learned enough about her younger sisters during their brief reunion to know that they had the propensity to live up to their reputation as being some of the silliest people in all of England. Her sister Jane she excluded from such an unflattering assessment. In addition, Mr. Collins remained a guest. Heaven only knew what a ridiculous spectacle he might make of himself in the wake of the noble addition to their family party.

Then there were her papa's sensibilities to consider. While Mrs. Bennet was willing to put aside any grievances against the Montlakes for the sake of putting her girls in the way of single, wealthy gentlemen, Elizabeth's papa could not be persuaded to grant anyone who bore the name Montlake any such consideration.

Not that he had been rude to Avery. Why, even Mr. Bennet would be the first to admit that it was not his place to disrespect the young duke. Had it been the former duke, Elizabeth would not swear her father would have been as agreeable. He hated the man for what he had done to the Bennet family, and he had sworn he would never forgive him, which brought Elizabeth's concern back to her mind. *How will Papa regard her ladyship?*

During the course of her ladyship's initial hours at Longbourn, everyone who habitually called on the Bennets did indeed call on them: all the Lucas ladies, Mrs. Greene, Mrs. Long, and anyone else who felt worthy of waiting on Lady Sophia — the woman who had raised Elizabeth as her own child. Mrs. Philips was there and, just as Elizabeth had come to expect, when her aunt was not quiet, she was very vulgar. Mr. Collins, feeling himself more than worthy of sitting next to Lady Sophia owing to his own lofty connections, did all he could to impress upon her his reason for being at Longbourn. He even supposed it was necessary to apologize for choosing the eldest Bennet daughter as the most deserving of his cousins to be his future wife as opposed to Elizabeth.

As soon as the last of Longbourn's guests were gone, Lady Sophia and Elizabeth excused themselves from the rest of the family party for time alone in Elizabeth's room. The two sat side by side on Elizabeth's bed, as had always been their wont when at home.

"Pray you're not horrified by my family's rather untoward behavior. As you have surmised, my Hertfordshire relations are nothing like the Gardiners."

"Elizabeth, my dear, you must never feel the need to apologize to me for the people who are your own flesh and blood."

Her spirits rising to playfulness, Elizabeth asked, "Not even Mr. Collins?"

"Not even Mr. Collins. I wager that were you to think of any number of our lofty aristocratic acquaintances, you would find they are not unlike your relations. Enjoying wealth and privilege does not alter the fact that people are very much the same wherever we go."

"Of course, you are correct. I shall endeavor to remember that the next time my idiot cousin delivers one of his preposterous speeches or my youngest sister parades herself before one of the officers."

"Indeed, it's human nature to want to prove one's significance. Not everyone goes about it in the same manner."

Elizabeth picked up her little doll with golden hair and blue eyes and started smoothing its dress.

Lady Sophia placed her hand on her chest. "I cannot believe you still carry this little doll with you on all your travels after all these years."

Elizabeth smiled and hugged her doll tightly. "I can never go anywhere without Jane. I'm afraid I would be lost without her."

Her ladyship smiled in turn. "Do you remember when your grandfather presented it to you? I shall never forget it. My, what a fuss you made that day. We were walking along hand in hand down the street and you tore away and raced over to the shop window, crying, "Jane — Jane!" You would not be satisfied until you pulled me inside and insisted the shopkeeper remove it from its window display."

Elizabeth toyed with the doll's golden ringlets while she listened to her ladyship recount the story she had heard so many times before. She could never hear enough how His Grace had finally relented amid her protests that persisted for days until, at last, the doll was hers. Indeed, she carried her Jane doll with her whenever she traveled. Not one night had passed in all the time she could remember that she did not give her beautiful doll a hug before closing her eyes to sleep.

Lady Sophia recalled the turmoil in her mind of late, wondering whether she should call on Elizabeth at Longbourn or allow her more time with her Bennet relations.

"Do you think she will object?" Her ladyship had asked Avery more than once. "You know how she has always protested my tendency to hover over her."

"That was when she was coming into her own and endeavoring to assert her independence. This is different. She loves you and she certainly wants you to be happy," Avery had affectionately reminded his mother.

Tears welled in Lady Sophia's eyes. She pushed a loosened tress of Elizabeth's hair aside and brushed a kiss atop her head. "I recall many nights of holding you in my arms to comfort you and feeling so helpless in the wake of your anguish. All that time, I never knew, I never supposed that your agony was owing to His Grace's own doing." She wiped a tear from her cheek. "I do not know that I will ever forgive him for what he did. I know I shall never forgive myself for my own complicity — however unwitting-ly."

"Pray do not blame yourself," Elizabeth cried. "You are completely innocent in all this. You could have no way of knowing the truth behind His Grace's wrongdoings."

"I believed what I wanted to believe. Having lost my husband and my precious little Bethany, the thought of facing yet another day became increasingly unbearable. Before I met you, I had no desire to carry on. Oh, Elizabeth, you changed all that. You came into my life at a time when I needed you most. I fell in love with you the moment I first laid eyes on you. You filled my life with joy and a new purpose." Again, she kissed Elizabeth atop her head. "You, my dear, mean the world to me."

Days later, Elizabeth was almost giddy, dancing about from one side of the room to the other. For reasons she would be hard pressed to explain without thinking too much about it, she was happier than she had been in a very long time, for she had it on good authority that Mr. Bingley was coming to Hertfordshire.

"Oh, what an excellent opportunity this is for our girls, specifically our Jane," Elizabeth heard her mama excitedly exclaim to her papa when she, too, learned of Mr. Bingley's imminent return.

Elizabeth recalled how happy Jane and Mr. Bingley were to see each other when they were all in Pemberley and how heartbroken her sister had been when Mr. Bingley took an early and rather abrupt leave. Jane believed it had to do with the gentleman's lack of regard for her, but Elizabeth thought differently.

Mr. Bingley's return can only mean one thing. He loves Jane, and he plans to make her an offer of marriage, Elizabeth quietly surmised, even at the risk of sounding like her mama.

She stopped in her tracks in consideration of what else Mr. Bingley's visit might entail. *It only makes sense, after all, that his friend Mr. Darcy might travel with him to Netherfield as well.* The last time Elizabeth saw Mr. Darcy was impressed upon her mind. *I more than hinted that a visit from him in Hertfordshire would meet with my approval.*

The suspense of not knowing if Mr. Darcy would be a member of Bingley's party was unbearable. She had no choice other than to wait and see, just like everyone else, for the prospect of receiving a letter from him was not very likely at all with his being a single gentleman and her being a maiden.

Elizabeth, in her confusion over the truth of her birth coming out, had been entirely remiss in writing letters to any of the people from her past life. That included Miss Georgiana Darcy, unfortunately. Any information she received about the goings on of the *ton*, she heard from Avery and Lady Sophia. As both of them were still reeling from the shock of what had befallen their family, they were frequently not of a mind to engage in discussions about anyone else's affairs.

Waiting and not knowing proved to be a trial for more than one of the ladies of Longbourn. It was incumbent upon Mrs. Bennet to hide from her guests just how excited she truly was over the prospect of Mr. Bingley's return — particularly Mr. Collins. Nothing was truly certain until the amiable, young, and exceedingly rich gentleman actually arrived. He may well have been married by now for all Mrs. Bennet knew. She did not intend to alienate one potential son-in-law on the uncertain hope that another, more desirable catch would soon take his place. Once Mr. Bingley returned, Mrs. Bennet would know how to act.

Chapter 12

Free to Indulge

Darcy had felt as though forces of the universe had been conspiring to keep him from arriving in Hertfordshire: a near fatal accident, raging fires amid the tenant homes, his cousin's schemes. He had endured it all, he now considered as he stepped down from the carriage. Finally, he enjoyed a breath of fresh air after what had been a rather uncomfortable trip, even in a large barouche as expensive as the one he owned.

Usually he would spend part of such a long trip like the one afforded from Derbyshire to Hertfordshire on horseback, but not this time. In fact, he did not arrange to bring his favorite stallion with him at all. Given the way his body ached, he did not suppose he would be riding very much for the next several weeks, if not months. Ah, but the ache in his heart would surely cease in a matter of hours and certainly over the course of a few days, if he could even bear to wait that long before calling on Longbourn.

Seeing Elizabeth's face will certainly make all that I have endured in traveling all this way worthwhile.

Moments later, Darcy espied his friend Charles Bingley bounding down the stone steps of his stately home. Darcy's smile vanished when he saw that his friend was not alone. Bingley's youngest sister, Miss Caroline Bingley, had also decided to venture outside and greet him.

Well, what did he expect? Charles Bingley and his single sister apparently were a package, one that he had learned to accept for the sake of his friendship with the younger man. *Rather tolerated,* he immediately considered. He then wondered if he and his own sister were closer in age, would she too have a habit of going with him almost every place he went? He smiled in spite of himself as he remembered that his cousin Lady Victoria, whom he loved as much as he would were she his sister, was his own version of Charles Bingley's sister what with her wont of spending so much time in his company.

This was no time to think of Lady Victoria. He was exceedingly annoyed with her for her uncharitable attitude towards Elizabeth. Unless she learned to curb her tongue, any times that Darcy spent with her in the future would be few and far between. Certainly, he would miss her dearly, but that was how it would be, and she would have no one to blame but herself. He endeavored to rid himself of any thoughts of Lady Victoria. He had spent more than enough time during the trip wondering what had happened to her. *Why does the prospect of my being in Hertfordshire and near Elizabeth meet with her disapprobation? Have I not made it perfectly clear to her what Elizabeth means to me, how there is no other woman for me but Elizabeth?*

By now, Darcy and his friend Charles Bingley were standing face to face. They accepted each other's outstretched hand.

Bingley's smile was as bright as the sun. "Darcy, old fellow, I am glad to see you have arrived safely and no worse for wear, I trust. I welcome you back to my home."

"It is my pleasure, my friend. I am glad to see you as well. When did you get here?"

Bingley said, "I arrived this morning. Overall, I would have to say it was a very pleasant trip. Of course, I only had to travel from town. After such a long journey from Derbyshire, I imagine you must be eager for a change in attitude."

Miss Bingley approached the gentlemen and curtsied. "Mr. Darcy, how lovely it is to see you again."

Darcy bowed slightly. "Miss Bingley. The pleasure is all mine."

Completely ignoring her brother and rather behaving as though Darcy was her special guest, she laced her arm through his and persuaded him to walk with her as they proceeded to the house.

"What a lovely time we shall have with all of us being together here at Netherfield Park just as we were last year. I only wish we might confine ourselves to our immediate party, for I so detest the much embellished pleasantries of Charles' country neighbors. But, alas, I suspect they will soon come calling. Let us make the most of our time together before the onslaught." She looked up at him and batted her eyelashes. "What say you, Mr. Darcy?"

"Perhaps you will give me leave to retire to my apartment for a while."

Bingley said, "Why, of course. You must take all the time you would like."

"I shall require just a short while to refresh myself after my long journey. I shall then meet you in— shall we say in the billiards room? It's been far too long since I bested you in the sport."

"I wager you will not meet with the same level of success that you have in the past."

Darcy chuckled. "You speak with a great deal of confidence, my friend, as though you know something I don't."

"I have a few tricks I've kept hidden, and you will not see them coming."

Caroline was not having any of this. "Oh, for heaven's sake, Mr. Darcy, you shall do no such thing as you suggest. The two of you shall have all the time in the world to enjoy your sport. We had much better all gather in the drawing room, for you will not believe my delicious news, Mr. Darcy. It has to do with that horrible Bennet family and one particular young woman whom we all know with her particularly fine eyes."

Darcy shook his head. *And so it begins.*

Miss Caroline Bingley's joy over Elizabeth's plight struck a chord of disdain in Darcy. She seemed outright giddy at the prospect of discussing what had unfolded. *That is her way, but does she expect me to rejoice in the unfortunate turn of events for people whom I hold dear to my heart?*

Darcy rolled his eyes to the ceiling as he made his way up the winding staircase to his apartment. *This is going to be a long day.*

Pleasing thoughts of her time with Mr. Darcy occurred to Elizabeth regularly of late. She supposed it had to do with the knowledge that Mr. Bingley was returning and her curiosity as to whether Darcy would be joining him. Now that she knew Mr. Darcy had indeed joined Bingley's party and he was but three short miles away, she could hardly wait to see him. The thought of seeing him again kept her awake most of the night, until finally she decided an early morning walk was the thing she needed to give her mind a most necessary diversion.

The morning air was chillier than she had expected. Elizabeth wrapped her arms around her shoulders. Walking along, she imagined what it would be like to be enveloped in Mr. Darcy's warm embrace.

If she were lucky, she might once again know what it was like to feel the touch of his lips on her face, her lips. Inwardly laughing at her wanton thoughts, she doubted either of them would allow things to progress that far during their initial encounter. *What if we were to meet on such a morning as this, when it would be just the two of us, free to indulge such fantasies?*

As the morning sun began poking through the clouds, a man she knew to be Darcy came from out of nowhere, much to Elizabeth's surprise as well as her delight. Who else could it be? No other man moved quite the way he did. She had not expected to see him so soon. She had meant for this to be an early morning walk where she would be all by herself, a quiet escape from Longbourn before her family stirred and commenced going about the new day.

The day before had passed, and no one from Netherfield had called on Longbourn. Mrs. Bennet was beside herself with worry, and she had even demanded that Mr. Bennet must call on Netherfield first in order that she and her daughters might then do the same. All the talk was that there were more people in the party other than Bingley, his two sisters, and his brother-in-law. Indeed, another illustrious person had joined the party — Mr. Darcy of Pemberley and Derbyshire.

Elizabeth was now seeing him alive and in person for the first time since they had parted at Pemberley with an unspoken promise between them. A tentative step from him, a pensive step from her, and moments later they were in each other's arms.

He had dreamed of seeing her for so long, and now here she was in his arms. Were they declared to each other, he would lift her face to his and kiss her lips, tenderly at first and then with abandonment. However, no such declaration existed between them, not yet, and even though there was no one but them at this beautiful place in the ever-constant rising sun, he knew he ought not to be holding her like this. Releasing her from his arms was beyond his power.

At length, her hands fell to her sides. Darcy, sensing the absence of her gentle touch, seized both her hands in his. They gazed into each other's eyes. "I have missed you."

Elizabeth spoke softly. "I have missed you too."

"Are those tears that I see?" He brushed his thumb across her chin. "Why are you crying?"

Freeing her hand, Elizabeth wiped her tears away. "You must forgive me, sir. It's just that we have been apart for so long, and I know I asked for this time so I might sort out my feelings about all that has happened in my life, but when my brother – when Avery – told me about your accident, I began to imagine all manner of horrible things. The worst one of all was that I might never see you again and yet here you are and I – I simply could not be happier and so you see, sir…"

How beautiful the ring of her voice sounded to him. The thought that his absence may have caused her pain was too much to bear. He placed his finger on her lips, thus interrupting her passionate declaration. "Yes, I am here. I am sorry you worried. I would have been here sooner were it not for the carriage accident. That was just one of many things that conspired to keep me from joining you here in Hertfordshire. None of that is important at this time. Instead, I simply want to hold you a while longer, and then we can talk. Will you allow me that pleasure?"

Elizabeth nodded and soon she was once again in his loving arms. Being in his arms that way felt just as it ought to. He was there. He had come all that way to be with her again. Not wanting to read more into his being there than was warranted, for she was still not confident he would accept her Bennet family, she decided now was not the time to do anything but enjoy being with him. No other man of her acquaintance had the power over her that this man commanded. It had been that way for as long as she had known him. Despite his accident, he appeared no worse for wear for indeed she had imagined all manner of things had befallen him, from the loss of a limb to scars marring his beautiful face, even blindness. Here stood the man as he had always been, and she counted herself happy.

Remembrances of the many intimacies they had shared in his dreams sought to intrude on their quiet moment, prompting Darcy to relinquish Elizabeth from his tender embrace.

They commenced walking along side by side, she with her arms folded in front of her, and he with his hands tucked behind his back.

"Despite my taking so long, you have to know I would allow nothing to keep us apart. I've vowed to wait for you until you are ready, but I can wait in Hertfordshire just as well as I can wait miles and miles away in Derbyshire." Stopping, he took her gloved hand in his and raised it to his lips. "How are you adjusting to your new circumstances?"

"All in all, my time has been wonderful, but it has not always been this way."

"How so?"

"You cannot imagine how hard it is for me to listen to the vile words that so easily flow from well-intentioned people's mouths about my grandfather — about His Grace. You see, I have not yet taught myself to hate him, despite what he has done." She searched Darcy's eyes for a modicum of much needed understanding. "Does that make any sense? Am I to be presumed as being mad because I do not hate His Grace?"

"I would not venture to say you are out of your mind, if that's what you mean, but one might expect a fair degree of anger towards the late duke on your part."

"Yes, I can admit to my share of anger. However, my anger does not translate into hate or even unshakeable resentment. The truth is I love him still, I miss him and I think of him every day."

"No doubt, you and your grandfather —" he paused " — His Grace, were exceedingly close. Pray, how do you get along with Mr. Bennet?"

"I love him — just as I love all my Bennet relations. Loving them is as easy as it is natural. They are by no means perfect. Of course, I do not need to tell you that. But, despite my family's imperfections, there is goodness in all of them, and I am so proud to call the Bennets my family."

Darcy rested his forehead against hers. It sounded if she were in no hurry to leave her new-found life behind, which he supposed must be a good thing for her in that she was happy, but it meant that much longer before the two of them could start their lives together in Derbyshire.

"I hope this does not meet with your displeasure, sir. It's just that I would like to suppose that I can talk to you more freely than I can with everyone else I know."

"Does that include Avery? I always supposed the two of you were very close."

"And we are, but there are some things I am not comfortable confiding in him."

"Things? What manner of things?"

"Things that have to do with our family — my place in the family."

"And yet you feel comfortable confiding in me?"

"Indeed, as you are as close to an impartial observer as I know. I do not get the sense that you would judge me harshly for sentiments that are not to be considered natural, if that makes any sense."

"I am glad you feel you can confide in me, Elizabeth, and I will not betray your confidence to anyone. You must never hesitate to speak your mind when you are with me. I am here for you. I shall be forever at your service."

Chapter 13

Speaking in Jest

A lone in Bingley's study, Darcy sat in a comfortable chair by the fireplace, dreaming of the enchanted morning he had spent with the beautiful woman with the most bewitching eyes. His thoughts were quite unlike what had actually unfolded between them during their chance meeting hours earlier. Just as had been the case during his laudanum-induced dreams at Pemberley, this dream was incredibly vivid.

Even in his dream state, he hated the thought that he might awaken any moment and find himself once again all alone — as always. He meant to enjoy this as long as he could. Kissing her about her face and her long, slender neckline would not do, for he felt too passionately not to leave evidence of their lovemaking, and thus he enfolded her in his embrace and lowered her to the ground. Enjoying the sensations of her soft body against his hard body, he commenced kissing her moist, pleasing lips – the sweetest wine he had ever tasted – and, at length, making her his in every way again and again.

Bingley's butler entered the room and thus interrupted Darcy's pleasing dream. "Mr. Thomas Bennet of Longbourn asks to see you this morning, sir."

Startled, after what he had just experienced, Darcy's first thought was that he ought to be on his knees beseeching Mr. Bennet for his daughter's hand in marriage. Allowing a second to clear his head, he stood from his chair and straightened his coat. "Please show the gentleman inside."

The butler did as he was bade, which gave Darcy a moment to ponder the reason he was receiving a visit from Elizabeth's father so early in the day. *Unless the gentleman is aware of our early morning chance encounter.*

Mr. Bennet entered the room. "Mr. Darcy, it is a pleasure to see you again."

"Indeed, sir. To what do I owe the pleasure of this visit?"

"It seems that I owe you a deep debt of gratitude, sir. I do not think I can ever repay you for being the means of reuniting my Lizzy with my family and me."

Darcy held up his hand. "You owe me nothing, sir."

"On the contrary — I owe you a great deal. Were these the days of ancient times long since gone by, I would be obliged to offer you your choice from among my five lovely daughters."

Darcy colored. He always supposed that Mr. Bennet was an odd mixture of whim and caprice, and someone who enjoyed making sport of others, but what if the older man knew more than he was letting on? Not that he would mind, for Darcy had every intention of marrying Elizabeth. However, he knew enough about her to know that now was not the time, for she had practically hinted as much when they parted earlier — she still needed time with her family before leaving them to spend her life with him.

Mr. Bennet must have read in Darcy's face his astonishment. "Fear not, young man, for I am merely speaking in jest. However, I have a favor to ask of you, and I pray you're of a mind to grant it."

"I shall do my best, sir. What is it that you wish to ask of me?"

"It has to do with the discussion we had when you and I talked all those months ago at Longbourn. Did you have any indication at the time that you were in possession of information that might lead to my daughter's return?"

Before Darcy could fashion a reply, Mr. Bennet said, "Now you must tell me all the particulars. When did you begin to suspect there might be a connection? My brother Gardiner told me what he could, but, with all due respect, his was no more than a second hand account laced with heightened emotions of joy and elation. I would much prefer to hear a less impassionate account from you."

Darcy offered the older man the seat opposite his and then did his best to oblige Mr. Bennet by telling him what he knew and when he knew it. Once he had satisfied all Mr. Bennet's questions, he was ready for a drink — but it was still early in the day for libations of the sort he had in mind.

When Mr. Bennet was ready to take his leave, he said, "I do not wish to speak out of turn, but I would like to suppose that your being here in Hertfordshire once more is not merely for the sake of visiting your friend Bingley at his country estate."

"Sir, you suppose correctly, but I am not at liberty to talk about that just now. Pray you understand."

"I respect your right to privacy, young man, but there is a particular adage that my wife is especially fond of, and it goes something like this: a single man in possession of a large fortune surely must be in want of a wife."

Peeping over his spectacles, Mr. Bennet continued, "Should your purposes for being here in Hertfordshire have anything at all to do with deciding upon a wife, I would say that you have my hearty consent to marry whichever of my daughters you choose."

Darcy and Bingley entered the parlor and saw that all the ladies of Longbourn were assembled. Included in their party was yet another familiar face — Lady Sophia Montlake.

Darcy truly had eyes for but one of the room's occupants. How pleased he was that the seat next to her was unoccupied. If only it were solely the two of them in the room. He would take her in his arms and recommence where they had left off earlier.

Elizabeth was thankful that her mama was on her best behavior that morning and she supposed that she was acting in that manner in deference to Lady Sophia's presence. If there was one thing that concerned Elizabeth, it was her mama's none too subtle reference earlier that Mr. Darcy's being in Hertfordshire meant that Kitty might indeed stand a chance at garnering his attention. Kitty protested that just as it was before, so it was now; she wanted nothing to do with the proud man.

Why would Mama suppose otherwise? And what would her mother think if she knew the true reason for Mr. Darcy's being there? A rather unsettling thought then occurred to her. Could her mother have been playing the part of an eager matchmaking mother when Mr. Darcy was first in Hertfordshire? Was that the reason he did not hold her in the highest esteem?

True, ever since he entered the room he had been the perfect gentleman. He did all that was required of him to convincingly act the part of an eager caller, but she knew him well enough to know that being in Longbourn with her mama and her sisters was the last place in the world he wanted to be, and the only reason he was even there was for her sake.

The guests had not long since arrived when Mrs. Bennet proposed that Jane and Bingley take a walk. She strongly hinted that Kitty walk with Mr. Darcy as well, but Kitty objected.

Lady Sophia proposed the perfect remedy. "Elizabeth will walk with Mr. Darcy, won't you, my dear?" It was perfect indeed, and the two couples were soon on their way.

Allowing Jane and Bingley to outpace them, when they were alone and at liberty to talk, Darcy said, "I always knew there was a reason I liked your mother Lady Sophia."

"Indeed, she was not too subtle just then."

"I owe her. I was eager to have you all to my-self if only for an hour or two."

"It seems I owe my gratitude to my sister Kit-ty."

"Yes, as you may have surmised, I am not your sister's favorite person."

"I know how you might change that—that is should you wish it."

"At the risk of sounding interested, pray how might that be?"

"Why, sir, you must lose your stuffy attire and don a bright scarlet coat."

He laughed. "If that is indeed the case, I will have to say that your sister is quite safe from me."

Darcy and Elizabeth were finally together again, which they both had been longing for. Perhaps Darcy had been longing for it more than Elizabeth, and with good reason, for, whereas she was the only thing missing in his life, Elizabeth had been missing an entire family – sisters, a mother, a father, aunts, uncles, and cousins – for the better part of hers. She had far more diversions to consume her every waking hour.

It stood to reason why she felt herself in need of more time to fill in the blanks of her life. Add to that the loneliness she felt in being away from the only home she truly knew with clarity and that she was mourning the duke's passing, despite all he had done in ripping her childhood apart. Her hand tucked neatly in the fold of Darcy's arm as they walked along, she said, "I cannot tell you what it means to me to know that you understand my feelings as they regard His Grace — that I would miss him still."

Darcy placed his free hand atop hers. "One's mind cannot command one's heart, and the fact is that the late duke earned a place in your heart long ago. Most of your memories of him are pleasant memories, and nothing you have learned about him since his passing has been sufficient to erase them. I see no harm in that."

Elizabeth rested her head on Darcy's arm, but only for a moment as she quickly remembered herself. While such a show of affection would go unnoticed were she walking along in that manner with Avery, such a gesture would raise eyebrows and set a few tongues wagging when done with someone so wholly unconnected to her as Mr. Darcy. Just the thought of it sent her mind back to her earlier question of how long he would wait before asking her to be his wife.

The thought that the question that had gone unasked when they parted ways in Pemberley might soon be asked, and an answer expected, then entered her mind.

Saying yes would mean my time here at Longbourn would soon come to an end. She was not certain she was ready to take her leave of her family so soon as an imminent marriage to a man who lived so far away would dictate.

Darcy did not fail to notice how Elizabeth was exercising extra measures to erect a barrier of sorts between them. He said, "I know you and I talked about your needing time with your family before committing yourself to a lifetime with me. I feel it incumbent upon me to tell you that my being here in Hertfordshire is in no way meant to interfere with that. I said I would wait for you and I intend to do just that. However, I must tell you what a pleasure it is being able to see you like this. I have thought of very little other than our being together, and as grateful as I am for this moment as well as for the intimacies we shared this morning, I do not mean to renege on that promise."

"Sir, I would be lying if I said I did not consider that you had grown tired of waiting and that you would wish to wait no longer. I am grateful for what you just told me. Hearing you reaffirm your promise to me is quite comforting, I assure you."

"Then we are both satisfied."

When the couples returned to Longbourn, Lady Sophia spoke softly to Elizabeth. "How did you enjoy your walk with Mr. Darcy, my dear?"

Elizabeth was rather shocked to discover that her mother was playing the role of the unabashed matchmaker. "I do not know that Mama appreciated your rather blatant attempt to thwart her favorite wish for my sister Kitty."

"That may indeed be the case, but Kitty certainly appreciated the gesture as did both you and your Mr. Darcy, I am certain."

Elizabeth lowered her voice. "*My* Mr. Darcy?"

Lady Sophia looked at the daughter whom she had reared for the greater part of her life knowingly. "Is he not, my dear?"

Indeed, the question hardly warranted an answer, for, seconds later, Darcy, having accepted the invitation to take a family dinner along with his friend Bingley, was once again by Elizabeth's side intent upon escorting her to the Bennets' dining parlor. Elizabeth spoke to him softly when she could. "Sir, I thought you and I had a tacit agreement that we would guard our behavior towards each other in order not to give rise to the expectation of an understanding between us."

"On the contrary — I promised I would wait until you were ready before I formally requested your hand in marriage. I did not promise I would pretend not to admire you. I couldn't even if I tried. You know not what you do to me."

Chapter 14

Lofty Connections

Now that Bingley was once again in the neighborhood, Mrs. Bennet had ceased her attempts to promote an alliance between the heir of Longbourn and her eldest daughter. Bingley was a much better catch. In fact, Mrs. Bennet likened his return to his coming for Jane.

This left four daughters from whom to choose to promote an advantageous alliance with the heir of Longbourn, for she was just as concerned as ever that, should Mr. Bennet die, she would be left alone in the world without a home to call her own.

Elizabeth could have her choice of any gentleman she wished, Mrs. Bennet was certain, owing to her lofty connections as well as her particularly large dowry of fifty thousand pounds. There was no need to waste her time finding a husband for her.

Mary, being the next in line, must certainly come to mind. "What an excellent wife our dear Mary shall make for Mr. Collins, do you not agree, Mr. Bennet?"

"My dear Mrs. Bennet, if you think that Mr. Collins shall not take umbrage to your first attempting to align him with Jane only to change your mind when a richer suitor comes to town and your subsequently attempting to substitute one sister for another then, by all means, do what you must."

"Oh, Mr. Bennet, how tiresome you can be when you're of a mind to be so. I only meant to suggest that Mary would make a more fitting wife for a parson."

"Pray what about my Lizzy? If you're bent on substituting daughters, is she not the next in line?"

"Lizzy is far too good for the likes of Mr. Collins. In fact, were I a betting woman, I would wager that Bingley's friend Mr. Darcy is fixed on Lizzy — which is a shame."

"A shame, my dear? Why would you say such a thing?"

"Mr. Darcy has over ten thousand pounds a year. What use has he for Lizzy's dowry? What use has she for all his wealth, although I do recall my sister Gardiner speaking of Pemberley's grandeur, but do you not suppose that a lord or a duke would live in such a home as well? Whereas Kitty would be an ideal match for Mr. Darcy, and such an alliance would satisfy my favorite wish for our next youngest daughter."

"Were that the gentleman's wish, I would have no objection to his marrying Kitty. He is a fine, upstanding young man, whom I would be honored to call my son, but I fear you are wasting your time wishing for such an alliance."

"Why do you say that? Our Kitty is every bit as lovely as our Lizzy."

"Oh, but you are missing a crucial piece in the puzzle. Kitty does not like Mr. Darcy, and I dare say he does not even know she's alive."

"Nonsense, Mr. Bennet. Even you will recall the way he looked at her when he first visited Hertfordshire last year. Those two may very well be destined for each other. We must simply do a better job of helping them on." Picking up her mending, Mrs. Bennet prepared to leave the room. "You wait and see. Our daughter shall be mistress of Mr. Darcy's magnificent home in Derbyshire before you know it."

Elizabeth and Darcy were walking along what was, by now, their favorite path, embroiled in a heated debate over her mama's scheme for her sister Mary. While Darcy was of the opinion that an alliance between Mary and Mr. Collins would make a most advantageous match, Elizabeth insisted her sister was worthy of a far better man. All of her arguments were insufficient to sway him. Elizabeth considered that he was so much like the late duke in that respect — overly fond of his own opinion. She told him as much.

Immediately afterward, she suffered a pinch of remorse. "I'm sorry, Mr. Darcy. Please forgive me."

"For what?"

"For suggesting that you are anything at all like the late duke."

"Elizabeth, you and I have talked about this. I know you loved him and you cherish his memory. I shall not consider it a slight against me in any way. He was a great man, albeit a flawed man. We are mere mortals — all of us. None of us is perfect."

Elizabeth's spirits rose to playfulness. "*The* Mr. Darcy of Pemberley and Derbyshire is not perfect. Do not allow Miss Caroline Bingley to hear you say that, or your cousin Lady Victoria either, for that matter."

She then went on to inquire, "How does she get along?"

"Miss Bingley?"

"No—no doubt she is exceedingly pleased what with your staying at Netherfield. I am asking about your cousin, Lady Victoria. How is she enduring your current separation?"

"You are aware that Lady Victoria and I reside miles apart? We are not nearly so inseparable as you seem to imply."

"Your behavior in London suggested otherwise. Rarely did I see you when I did not see her last Season."

"Well, I suppose you have a point there. While we are discussing my cousin, you ought to know that she spent a great deal of time at Pemberley during my recuperation from the accident."

"Will you forgive me if I say I am a bit envious of her in that regard? I should have liked to have been the person who cared for you all those weeks."

"Trust me when I say that I would have much preferred it was you. The thought of you is what sustained me, and rarely did I close my eyes that I did not see your face. And when I slept, I believe I dreamed only of you."

"You dreamed about me, Mr. Darcy?"

"Indeed—often."

"Do you care to tell me more?"

Darcy could feel the color rise in his face and frissons of excitement arousing him. "Now is not the time to speak of such things."

"Oh, and when will be the proper time?"

Darcy placed his hands upon her face. Leaning, he lifted her chin and brushed his thumb across her lips. How he wanted to show her what he recalled of his dreams. He leaned closer still and spoke softly into her ear. "Not only will I tell you, but I also mean to spend a fair amount of time showing you when we are married."

Chapter 15

Into the Shadows

By the time Darcy espied Miss Bingley heading his way, at a gathering at Lucas Lodge, it was too late. "It seems that the heinous Montlake scandal has not diminished your admiration of Eliza's fine eyes one bit," she said.

"And why should it? In essentials, she is every bit the same as she ever was."

"Perhaps, but what respectable gentleman would want to attach himself to such a scandal? Although I do understand she has a substantial dowry, which must surely tempt a lesser man. I understand an old acquaintance of yours is quite a favorite among the Bennet daughters and that he and Eliza are said to spend prodigious time in each other's company. From what I can discern, she is his favorite."

Darcy did not know which part of Miss Bingley's gossiping he found more disconcerting: that she was making light of Elizabeth's situation or that he would only encourage her with his next question. Still, his curiosity to know who was spending time with Elizabeth would not be repressed.

"An old acquaintance of mine?"

"Indeed. Lt. George Wickham."

"Wickham!" *What is that cad doing in Hertford-shire?* "George Wickham—a lieutenant? Surely your sources are mistaken."

"Indeed I am not! I have seen the gentleman in Meryton with my own eyes. My sister and I were riding in our carriage and I looked out the window. There he stood with another officer, surrounded by a hoard of foolish young ladies eager to garner his approbation."

Darcy had heard enough, and he pardoned himself from Miss Bingley's company with a slight nod. There was but one person with whom he wished to speak. He found her standing with his friend Bingley and Miss Bennet.

Bingley said, "Darcy, it is so nice of you to join us. You must help us settle a debate that finds me outnumbered by these two lovely ladies."

"Perhaps another time," said Darcy. "I find myself much in need of refreshment. Pray you will join me, Miss Elizabeth." His speech sounded much more like a directive rather than an invitation.

Elizabeth accepted his proffered arm and excused herself from Bingley and Jane's company with a polite smile. Darcy spoke not a word until they were alone on the balcony.

Turning to face her, he said, "Wickham, Elizabeth?"

"What about Mr. Wickham, sir?"

"Is it true that you have been spending time in his company in my absence?"

"I beg your pardon, sir, but I hardly understand the question, and I surely do not abide your tone. What does your presence, or lack thereof, have to do with whose company I choose to spend my time in?"

"Well, there is a bit of subterfuge if ever there was an intention to avoid one's question."

"Sir, you speak as if I mean to hide something from you, which I assure you is not what I am about. As for the substance of your question, yes, I have renewed my acquaintance with Mr. Wickham since my return to Hertfordshire."

"Surely you will recall my admonishment to you to be wary of that gentleman."

"Yes, I believe that was when you and I first made each other's acquaintance. However, I will tell you precisely what I told Avery when he attempted to do the same. I will keep my own counsel as regards Mr. Wickham. He is a great favorite wherever he goes. Why should I allow your sentiments to fashion my own?"

"Wickham is blessed with such happy manners that he is sure to make friends wherever he goes — whether he is capable of keeping them is less certain."

"I know that he has been so unfortunate as to lose your good opinion, as well as Avery's, but, as I said, that can have nothing to do with me."

"It ought to."

"Surely you do not allow my opinion of others to inform your views, sir."

"In what regard?"

Elizabeth crossed her arms. "For one, I do not like your cousin Lady Victoria Fitzwilliam, and you seem to think she walks on water."

"That's a lofty charge. I am well aware of my cousin's faults." *More now than ever,* he considered. "However, I will not allow you to distract me from my purpose. I am not at all comfortable with your spending any time in Wickham's company."

"You truly are serious about this?"

"And why wouldn't I be? The man is not fit for polite society." At that moment, two officers walked past Darcy and Elizabeth. His voice filled with annoyance, Darcy said, "I am surprised he is not slithering about this evening."

"Mr. Wickham was called away to town on matters of business before you arrived in Hertfordshire. He is to return in a fortnight."

Darcy said, "You seem to take an eager interest in that gentleman's comings and goings."

"Nonsense, Mr. Darcy. Being privy to such a fact is hardly the same as being eagerly concerned." She placed her hand on his arm. "What is the source of all this acrimony? I know you do not like the man and I accept that, just as you accept the fact that I do not like your cousin. If I did not know better, I would say this is more than dislike, but jealousy — which, I might add, does not become you."

His countenance softened considerably. He took her hand and raised it to his lips. He then kissed her wrist, sending frissons of pleasure laced with anticipation through her body. Darcy pulled Elizabeth into the shadows. "The thought of your spending time with that scoundrel, with any man, for that matter — " He brushed his lips against hers. "The thought of another man gazing into your amazing eyes — " He swept his lips along her neckline. "Thinking such thoughts as these does things to me."

Elizabeth, who loved being so close to him, thought better of where they were. Not truly wanting to escape the magic of his kiss, she placed her hands on his broad chest and lingered a second or two before gently pushing him away. "You know I would never allow such intimacies with anyone other than you." She pursed her lips teasingly. "If you and I do not cease and return to the others, my papa might insist that you marry me."

"I want us to be married—I want to take you away from all this."

"I am not ready to leave any part of this behind."

He ceased his amorous ministrations. Biting his lower lip, savoring the sweet taste of hers, he said, "Of course not." He took her hand in his and gave it a gentle squeeze. "Promise me you will meet me in the morning."

Elizabeth smiled. She nodded.

Releasing her hand, Darcy said, "You must return. I shall join you momentarily, my love."

Darcy used his time alone for two purposes: one to allow his ardor to cool and, two, to contemplate his options where George Wickham was concerned. *He is sure to return to Hertfordshire soon, and, no doubt, he will resume his attentions towards Elizabeth. It will not do.* Other than his cousin Colonel Fitzwilliam, Darcy had spoken to no one about what happened in Ramsgate. *He tried and failed to secure Georgiana's dowry. What is to stop him from attempting to get his hands on Elizabeth's fortune? There is no telling what that scoundrel would do to bring about such a prospect.* Darcy's choice was clear. He needed to tell Elizabeth everything about George

Wickham. *I see no other way to open her eyes to his true character before it is too late.*

Early the next morning, Darcy waited for Elizabeth in their usual place. When she came into view, he noticed she was not alone. Moments later, when they were face to face, he said, "This is not a complaint, but you might have told me that your companion would be with you this morning."

She huffed. "Her being here is not by my design, I assure you." Indeed, Elizabeth was quite surprised to see Miss Greene waiting by the doorway to accompany her on her morning walk. Insisting that she must be allowed to do her job properly, she would not take no for an answer. She did not say that the Duke of Dunsmore would be most seriously displeased to know that Elizabeth had a habit of arising before the rest of the household and taking long, solitary walks about the countryside, but those words were buried in her tone. At least she had agreed to give Elizabeth a bit of privacy, which explained her having settled herself some distance away, once Darcy was in sight.

Darcy said, "I suppose it is just as well, your being accompanied when you are away from Longbourn, especially now that the likes of George Wickham are lurking about."

"Pray we will not spend what little time we have together this morning discussing that gentleman again. I thought we had reached an agreement — you hate him, and I do not. Further discussion is inconsequential."

"No—I am not content to leave it at that. I need you to understand the basis for my dislike of the man, and then I trust you will know how to act."

"Mr. Darcy, you ought to know that Mr. Wickham attempted to poison my mind against you earlier on in our acquaintance. I would not hear a single word spoken against you. Do you not suppose I ought to give him the same courtesy?"

"I would like to think your allegiance to me does not compare to any loyalty you may feel towards that scoundrel."

"You are correct, sir. As you are determined to persuade me of the gentleman's unworthiness, I am obliged to listen, so long as you will give me leave to think what I will afterward."

"Elizabeth, it is important to me that what I am about to confide in you be regarded with the utmost discretion, for it has to do with my sister, Georgiana. You know enough of my family's history to know that my father loved George Wickham." Darcy went on to convey to Elizabeth the basis of his abhorrence of the vile man.

What an unfortunate circumstance that had been—one he wished to forget. "Georgiana had been in a Mrs. Younge's care for nearly a year, ever since I took her from school and put her in her own establishment. The entire time, Mrs. Younge had presided over the establishment without incident and thus given me the impression that she was truly a decent woman, as all her credentials had advised.

"I had no idea she had a prior acquaintance with George Wickham. Undoubtedly by design, that despicable man followed Georgiana and Mrs. Younge to Ramsgate last year. By the latter's connivance and aid, Wickham so far recommended himself to Georgiana, whose affectionate heart retained a strong impression of his kindness to her as a child, that she persuaded herself she was in love with him and she consented to an elopement.

"What a travesty such a scandal might have wrought upon my family had I not arrived when I did. Georgiana, unable to support the idea of disappointing me by acting in a manner that she knew must certainly grieve and offend me, acknowledged the whole scheme.

"I knew precisely how to act. Wickham's chief object was, without question, Georgiana's fortune of thirty thousand pounds. Still, I cannot help supposing the hope of revenging himself on me for what he continues to insist was my ill use of him regarding my father's final wishes and the living in Kympton was a strong inducement. Wickham's revenge would have been complete indeed."

How wretched Elizabeth now felt having defended a man who was capable of such wickedness. "I am very sorry for all that your sister had to endure as a result of Mr. Wickham's cruel intentions."

"Pray now you understand why I find the thought of your spending time in his company so objectionable. He does not warrant your approbation or your kindness."

"Of course, in my defense, I always supposed that you two were practically family, and in time the gulf between you would be healed."

"I dare say that will never happen. My greatest wish is that I never lay eyes upon him again, although I know the chances of that are next to impossible with his being in the militia encamped just outside of Meryton."

"Is this your way of saying that you plan to remain in Hertfordshire for an extended amount of time, Mr. Darcy?"

"Indeed, I do. I know you need this time with your family, but I need you — I need to be able to see you and spend time with you every day." He took her hand in his and brushed a kiss across her knuckles.

"I owe you an apology where my cousin is concerned as well. I ought to have heeded your advice, for I suspect her feelings for me are vastly different from those I had long supposed."

"Oh?"

"Indeed. However, I have made it perfectly clear to her that, when the time is right, I plan to make you my wife."

Chapter 16

An Unspoken Commitment

Darcy had not been in Hertfordshire for a fortnight before receiving an urgent missive from his uncle, the Earl of Matlock, to return to Derbyshire post haste to attend to an important family matter concerning his cousin Lady Victoria.

The letter was rather cryptic, for it spoke of her ladyship's ill health. Her situation demanded that Darcy return to her side and do what was right by his cousin.

Darcy's pacing nearly wore a trench in the garden path. What was his uncle's purpose in summoning him back to Derbyshire? Why wasn't the earl more forthcoming as to the reason? Certainly, if his cousin needed him, then he would be there, but some explanation as to the nature of her affliction would surely have sufficed.

Now, I am left to wonder, to hope, and to pray her situation is not grave. Lady Victoria is a young, healthy woman. Surely she will recover from whatever malady has befallen her.

Sweeping his fingers through his hair, he exhaled a frustrated breath. *If I have but one regret, it is that my time here with Elizabeth has come to an end far sooner than I would have wished.*

Indeed, and the fact of the matter was he had no way of knowing how long it would be before he would be able to return. It would help if he had some idea of what his cousin was suffering. Darcy had a startling feeling he did not wish to know. They had not parted on the best of terms because his determination to be in Hertfordshire had indeed met with his cousin's great displeasure.

Did Victoria tell her father that she thinks she is in love with me? Is that what this is about? What if she is not ill at all, but she has instead fabricated some malady in order that I might leave Elizabeth? Pray my cousin has not taken to deception.

Then, as he began to consider the alternative that she was indeed ill, he supposed he much preferred that she was not. A lie he could abide, even if it was the means of tearing him away from Elizabeth's side, but Lady Victoria's ill health was something he could hardly contemplate without despair.

The instant Darcy saw Elizabeth heading his way he set off to meet her. "My dearest Elizabeth, thank you for meeting me like this."

"I can imagine that whatever you have to say is of grave importance else you would not have resorted to such subterfuge," she said, referring to the brief missive neatly hidden inside a book that was delivered to her from Netherfield. She looked at him and noticed the sad turn of his countenance. "What is the matter? You look as though you have lost your best friend."

"I would say you are not too far from the truth."

"You are beginning to worry me, Mr. Darcy."

"Forgive me, for it is not my intention to lay my troubles at your feet."

"Then you will admit that something is terribly wrong. What is it?"

"I had to meet you here today, for what I have to say is not something that could be conveyed in a letter and it is not something that I wanted to discuss in the company of others. I received a letter from my uncle, Lord Matlock. An express rider delivered it first thing this morning. The earl said that my cousin Lady Victoria has suffered a drastic change in health."

"Oh dear, did he say what is the matter?"

"He did not, but he did say that I owed it to my cousin to come to Matlock without delay."

"This sounds grave indeed."

"Pray it is not, but I have to do as he says. If my cousin needs me, then I ought to be there."

"Of course."

"You understand that I would not leave Hertfordshire otherwise."

"Yes, family is important. You must go and do what you must to be of comfort to your cousin."

Darcy walked over to Elizabeth and placed his hands about her arms. "You truly are wonderful. I thought you might be upset over my leave-taking so soon after I arrived. I had planned to stay for another month, at least."

"I understand that you must do what you must do. You need not worry over me. Go; be by your cousin's side and know that I will be here waiting for your return."

"Before I leave, I wish to give you this." Darcy retrieved a silk pouch from his pocket. Opening it, he removed a gold necklace that held a single, lustrous, white pearl. "I want there to be more than an unspoken commitment between us."

Pleasantly surprised, she obliged his silent beckoning to place the necklace around her neck. He lingered, sending waves of excitement throughout her body. Feathering soft kisses in his wake, he said, "I love you, Elizabeth."

Bingley was obliged to be in town on business for a week and, thus, he was away from Netherfield Park when Darcy received the letter from the Earl of Matlock. As dissatisfied as Miss Bingley and Bingley's other sister, Mrs. Hurst, were that Mr. Darcy would no longer be a member of their country party, the news did not meet with their complete displeasure.

"Was Mr. Darcy's being here not the reason for all of our being here? I cannot imagine staying here in this dreary place now that he has returned to Derbyshire. This is the perfect time for us to escape to town."

Principally occupied in playing with her bracelets and rings, Mrs. Hurst said, "Caroline, I should imagine Charles will be terribly disappointed if he does not have a chance to settle things with Miss Bennet properly. You know how disappointed he was over our manner of leave-taking after the ball last year."

"Nonsense, Louisa! We had every right to act as we did. We are not our brother's prisoners and, should he take offense to what we have done, he can come here and open the house himself. I would much rather return to town and prepare for the upcoming Season."

"But what shall we tell Miss Bennet?"

"Why should we tell her anything? Why should we give her any cause to believe that she is more worthy of such a consideration than the rest of our brother's neighbors?"

"Caroline, you know very well that she is. You know that Charles fancies himself half in love with her. She might one day be our sister were he to return and make her an offer, which, no doubt, he may very well plan to do."

"That is all the more reason for us to take our leave, for he is far less likely to return to an empty house. I shall simply write a letter to Jane and tell her that we have decided to go back to town — as an act of courtesy, if you will."

Two days later, Jane was sitting all by herself in the garden when Elizabeth came upon her. She held a letter in her hands as she fought to hold back the tears that threatened to escape from her eyes.

Elizabeth said, "Jane, I am surprised to find you here. When I did not see you in the house, I supposed your Mr. Bingley had called and the two of you were enjoying a walk to Oakham Mount." A closer observation revealed her dearest sister's anguish. "Jane, what is the matter? Have you been crying?"

Wiping her eyes, Jane tucked the letter into her pocket. "No, I mean yes … I mean no. Oh, you must not worry over me, Lizzy. I sometimes suffer the occasional bout of melancholy. I assure you there is no cause for concern."

"Jane, there is no need to put on a brave front with me. You cannot convince me that there is nothing wrong. Why, the last time I came across you looking so forlorn was when we were together at Pemberley." The source of Jane's sadness then dawned upon Elizabeth. "Has this anything to do with Mr. Bingley? Have the two of you suffered some misunderstanding?"

Jane said, "Mr. Bingley is not here."

"Are you saying that you expected him to arrive at Longbourn and he is tardy? I am sure he has a good explanation."

"That is not what I am saying at all. You see, Lizzy, Mr. Bingley is not in Hertfordshire. He has decided to remain in London."

"How can that be when he promised he would take a family dinner here this evening? Mama has been planning for this occasion for weeks. Did Mr. Bingley give a reason for his decision to remain in London?"

"I have not seen or heard from the gentleman."

"Then how do you know he has no plans to return to Hertfordshire?"

"His sister Caroline told me in a letter. It arrived not long ago."

"Is that what you were reading when I came upon you? Exactly what did she say in her letter?"

Jane pulled the letter from her pocket and handed it to her sister. "Here it is — you may read it for yourself."

Elizabeth read the letter rather hastily. Her disbelief that a gentleman as charming and amiable as Mr. Bingley was capable of such thoughtlessness steadily increased. "If what Caroline said is true that means her brother has indeed decided to remain in town. But why did he lead us all to believe that he intended to return?"

"Why does he do anything that he does is a better question. Let us face it, Lizzy; Mr. Bingley simply does not care for me in the way a man ought to care for a woman who has touched his heart."

"I do not believe it, Jane. Mr. Bingley loves you more than he knows. A person need only observe the way he looks at you when he thinks no one is watching him."

"You do not know how much I wish that were true, but the fact is that this is the third time he has left my company without taking a proper leave and each time with no promise of ever returning — not at all like your Mr. Darcy. Mr. Darcy is a man who suffers every symptom of love for you, and he proves it every day by his actions. Do you know what I would give to enjoy that kind of loyalty and devotion?"

"You have that in Mr. Bingley."

"If only what you expound was true, but you and I both know it is not. Trust me, Lizzy, I do not mean to disparage Mr. Bingley in any way, for I believe he is a decent man who is easily persuaded by his sisters. The better I know them, the more I detect in them an air of intolerance towards our family."

All objections to the contrary would have proved quite disingenuous on Elizabeth's part. Her history with the Bingley sisters had taught her that they not only disdained the Bennets, owing to their lack of fortune and want of connections, they felt this way about everyone whom they deemed their inferiors.

They were, in fact, very fine ladies, not deficient in good humor when they were pleased, nor in the power of making themselves agreeable when they chose it, but they were proud and conceited. They were rather handsome, had been educated in one of the first private seminaries in town, had a fortune of twenty thousand pounds each, were in the habit of spending more than they ought, and of associating with people of rank.

They were, therefore, in every respect entitled to think too well of themselves and meanly of others. They were of a respectable family in the north of England, a circumstance more deeply impressed on their memories than that their brother's fortune and their own had been acquired by trade.

Elizabeth never liked them before, and she liked them even less now. *If Mr. Bingley truly is so easily persuaded by the likes of those two to subject Jane to heartbreak and disappointed hopes, then I shall suppose he is a fool who is unworthy of my sister after all.*

His True Character

Both Darcy and his uncle looked stunned when Lady Victoria walked into the room. Standing, Darcy regarded her from head to toe. He said nothing.

Lord Edward Fitzwilliam, an august gentleman, did not look kindly upon the interruption. "Victoria, what are you doing here? This matter is between Darcy and me."

"You are discussing my future, no doubt the particulars of my marriage settlement. I insist upon being here."

"Marriage settlement," Darcy said, his voice laced with disbelief. "You're getting ahead of yourself."

"It is a pleasure to see you too, Cousin."

Taking his seat, Darcy resumed his former attitude.

"Darcy and you are not of the same mind, I fear. He insists that your accusations are merely the result of desperation on your part."

What else could it be? To have behaved in the manner that might reasonably find him in such a position surely would have required rather active participation on his part. Darcy had no memory of ever being with his cousin in that way. It had to be a mistake. He mentioned as much to Lady Victoria and thus there ensued a litany of retorts back and forth.

The earl found himself in the impossible position of not knowing who or what to believe. The two cousins' bickering was not helping. How untenable the situation was shaping up to be. He knew his nephew to be a decent and honorable man. He had never known him to lie, even as a child.

The earl, out of love for his daughter and out of respect for his only nephew, stood. "Please, this is enough!" He gave his waistcoat a sharp tug. "I know not what to believe. A union between the two of you would meet with no objection from me, but it must not come about amid untruths and misunderstandings. I will leave the two of you to allow you to settle this confusion." He pointed a finger at his nephew. "But hear me, Darcy, if what my daughter accuses you of is true, you *will* marry her." He then turned to Lady Victoria. "And believe me, Daughter, if this all turns out to be a ruse, I will be obliged to lock you up for the rest of your life."

Darcy sat there in utter and complete disbelief. The prospect that he may have satisfied his baser needs with his cousin – even as an unwilling participant and even in a drug-induced haze – was unfathomable. It could not be true. He would not believe it unless and until confirming evidence presented itself, and then he would know how to act.

When they were alone, he stood and walked to the window. "How is this to be endured?"

His cousin's response fell silent to his ears. At length, he brushed his hands over his face, wishing to block out whatever his cousin was saying. Only one thought consumed him.

He muttered aloud, "What must Elizabeth think when she hears of any of this?"

Lady Victoria's mouth gaped. "Elizabeth— Elizabeth! Do you know how tired I am of hearing your every sentence begin and end with that horrid woman's name?" She placed her hands about her waist. "How is this to be endured, you ask? Well, you might try closing your eyes when we are together as man and wife and pretend that *I* am Elizabeth. It seems to have worked for you before!"

With that, Lady Victoria turned and raced from the room.

Where Elizabeth had once found Mr. Wickham to be an amiable companion, now knowing what she knew about his true character, Wickham's company only served to annoy rather than please her. *How is such a man to be trusted?*

Having no reason to doubt the veracity of Mr. Darcy's charge against George Wickham, Elizabeth regarded him as calculating and duplicitous. She and Wickham were standing among a crowd when, one by one, the others took their leave, and then only the two of them remained.

"I understand my old friend Darcy finally saw fit to take his leave of Hertfordshire."

"Indeed, family affairs dictated his return to Derbyshire."

"I doubt his being called away met with any great disappointment. The Darcy I know could hardly be very contented in such a place as Hertfordshire. I suppose your being here must have been the inducement for his staying as long as he did. I know how much you like him."

"I have never made it a secret how much I admire Mr. Darcy. With his having confided in me some rather disconcerting information about his young sister, I must say my admiration for him has increased one-hundred fold. Moreover, anyone whom he regards as his enemy I am inclined to regard as my own." She looked at him pointedly. "I trust you take my meaning, sir."

Having forced Elizabeth to say what gave no one any pain but himself, Wickham then departed.

Jane joined her sister immediately thereafter. "Lizzy, what have you done to Mr. Wickham? I do not recall ever seeing him so dispirited. Pray the two of you did not argue over his sudden interest in Miss King?"

"Oh, if that were only the case, Jane," said Elizabeth, taking her sister by the hand. "Come and take a stroll in the garden with me. What I am about to convey requires the utmost privacy." Elizabeth had not told anyone what Darcy had confided in her about his family's history with George Wickham. Darcy had placed a great deal of trust in her discretion, and Elizabeth was not about to betray that trust. Still, she felt it incumbent upon her to share what she could about the exact nature of the lieutenant's character with her closest sister. Thus resolved to omit every particular of Mr. Darcy's account as it related to his sister, Miss Darcy, Elizabeth conveyed the history between the two gentleman in such a way that Jane would have no doubt that Wickham was not the epitome of goodness he pretended to be.

What a shock this was for poor Jane, who only meant to see the good in everyone. Should anyone falter in that regard, Jane was always the first to reason it away in the best possible light. "Poor Mr. Wickham! There is such an expression of goodness in his countenance and such openness and gentleness in his manner. However, I know Mr. Darcy to possess all those agreeable traits as well. You mentioned that they were raised together — that they were the best of friends at one time. Could this merely be a misunderstanding between them that simply wants a measure of forgiveness on both their parts?"

"Jane, I always supposed the same, and that is the reason I was willing to give both gentlemen the benefit of the doubt. It is more than Wickham's repeated lies about Mr. Darcy's denying him the living that he says ought to have been his — much more. I am not at liberty to say more, but you must trust me when I say that Wickham's behavior towards Mr. Darcy and those closest to him is both shocking and appalling. Wickham is not to be trusted, and I wonder if I ought to make our acquaintances in general understand his character."

Jane paused a little and then said, "He has given us no occasion for exposing him so dreadfully. Perhaps it ought not to be attempted."

"You are quite right. Mr. Darcy did not authorize me to make any part of his communication public, and if I endeavor to make people aware of Wickham's conduct without substantial proof, who would believe me?"

Jane nodded. "What's more, to have his errors made public might ruin him forever. I contend he is anxious to re-establish his character. Surely his interest in Miss King, should it lead to an alliance, will go a long way in helping him in that regard. Let us do nothing that would make him desperate."

Thus resolved, the two sisters headed back inside the house. What a mixture of chaos and heightened emotions greeted them upon their return. Mr. Collins had done the unthinkable. He had spurned all the Bennet daughters and offered his hand in marriage to Miss Charlotte Lucas. What Elizabeth found most disconcerting was the fact that her intimate friend had accepted the foolish man.

Mrs. Bennet blamed herself. "Oh, why did I pin all my hopes on that inconstant Mr. Bingley? My Jane might have been Mr. Collins's wife by this time had it not been for my impatience to see her settled as the next mistress of Netherfield."

Mrs. Bennet blamed Mr. Collins himself. "How dare he come around proclaiming his intention of choosing a wife from among his fair cousins and lapping up all of Longbourn's hospitality when all he actually meant to do was to take a full and thorough accounting of his future home and make laughing stocks of us all. Oh! I knew there was a reason I always detested the man."

Most of all, Mrs. Bennet blamed Charlotte Lucas. "That scheming conniver has always been an artful sort of girl. She and her family have always been all for what they can get. I knew she had a secret agenda for calling on Longbourn as often as she did; parading herself in front of a man whom she knew was destined to marry one of my daughters, and using her feminine arts and allurements to steal him away. And now I find out that such a woman is to be the future mistress of Longbourn." Fanning herself profusely with her linen handkerchief, Mrs. Bennet threw herself on the sofa. "I believe I shall go distracted."

Sitting in his study, slowly imbibing his drink, and staring at the fiery flames dancing about the fireplace, Darcy endeavored to piece together what might have happened during his recovery. What if his vivid dreams were not dreams at all, but events that had actually unfolded during his drug-induced state?

I have never supposed my cousin to be conniving and calculating. He then recalled that farce of a letter she gave him — the one that was meant to fool him into believing that Elizabeth never wished to see him again. It had indeed given him cause to know that his cousin was not above fabrication and deceit.

What if this is her final act of desperation? To accuse me of fathering her unborn child, which she may or may not be carrying? As he began to question whether she was indeed with child, but someone else was the father, the worst possible scenario conceivable came to his mind. *What if what she is accusing me of is true? Then all my hopes and dreams for a future life with Elizabeth would be no more.* He would stand by his cousin rather than allow her to suffer shame and derision, even if it were of her own making. He cared for her too much to do otherwise.

Thoughts of the light and pleasing figure of the woman who truly held his heart came to mind. Standing, he walked to his desk. He could no longer put off that which he knew he was obliged to do.

Days later, what a surprise it was for Elizabeth to be receiving a letter from Miss Georgiana Darcy, especially after having gone so long with no correspondence at all between them. Her pleasure soon surrendered to panic that another tragedy may have befallen Mr. Darcy. Calmness ensued when, upon opening the missive, she saw that it was from Mr. Darcy himself.

She did her best to hide her joy from the rest of the family as she quickly made her way to her room to read his letter in privacy.

Each carefully written line disquieted Elizabeth. The missive was hardly written in the spirit of an absent lover's hand. Indeed, the last part concerned her. Skipping the initial pleasantries that were to be expected in a letter from one whom she had known for so long a duration, she read the disconcerting part once more:

"Though disguise in any manner is my abhorrence, there are times when such desperate measures are the only means available. This is one of those times.

I am afraid there has been a grave misunderstanding, the importance of which has the potential to alter the course of my life forever. It has to do with my cousin Lady Victoria Fitzwilliam.

It is not something I am at liberty to discuss by letter, but please be assured I am more than eager to discuss it with you. I have been unable to return to Hertfordshire as soon as I had hoped, but believe me when I say I will come to you and explain everything as soon as I can. Yours, FD"

Ponder the Matter

Being surrounded by a household full of relatives was something that distinguished this Christmas from Christmases gone by for Elizabeth. In addition to her immediate family members, the Gardiners were visiting from town. If she had thought that her youngest sisters were silly before, they were even more so now, only this time the gaieties afforded by the Season perfectly allowed for it. Elizabeth's little cousins, the Gardiners' four children, brought out the silliness in everyone.

A relatively young woman in comparison to Mrs. Bennet and Mrs. Philips, Mrs. Gardiner's business, when she was not describing the newest fashions and various goings on in London, was listening. First, there were Mrs. Bennet's fervent complaints of being ill-used by so many to sort through, which must surely command a great deal of time and a fair degree of patience. Then the younger girls demanded their fair share of their aunt's attention. When, at last, it was Elizabeth's turn, she and Mrs. Gardiner contrived to be alone in the east parlor.

Sitting next to her niece, Mrs. Gardiner said, "I understand from your mother, there have been any number of suitors parading about Longbourn of late."

"No doubt Mama was lamenting her inability to land all of them as husbands for my sisters and me."

"I believe what pained her most was that the heir of Longbourn chose a bride other than one of her daughters."

"Ah, Mr. Collins."

"Yes, I understand his express purpose in coming here was to choose a bride from his fair cousins and yet he chose Miss Charlotte Lucas."

Elizabeth nodded. "Indeed, you can well imagine how much it pains Mama to have to endure such a prospect as someone other than herself being the mistress of Longbourn."

"My sister affirms that the young lady conspired to steal him away and that her purpose in befriending you was merely to have a good excuse to always be at Longbourn."

"It is true that Charlotte and I have become rather fast friends. I cannot ascribe such nefarious motives to her as does Mama. While I did not at first like the idea of Charlotte accepting my hideous cousin's hand, I have been given to consider that Charlotte is practical. With so many younger siblings, she found herself a burden to her family and now she will be mistress of her own home. Besides all that, I am much relieved that Mr. Collins did not go through with Mama's initial scheme and offer his hand to Jane or Mama's second scheme to offer his hand to Mary. I fear either of the two of them would have accepted him, and I have always supposed both of my sisters deserve better."

"I suppose we have Mr. Bingley's visit to thank for sparing Jane such a prospect."

"I fear that is one of the few benefits that arose from his visit. His coming was certainly a cause for anticipated hopes, but I am afraid his leave-taking was yet another means of disappointing Jane."

"I am sorry to see Jane so disheartened once again over Mr. Bingley's inconstancy. He seems like such an amiable young man, but I have only met him once when we were all at Pemberley. His brief stay allowed little time to sketch his true character."

"I would say he is very agreeable. He is handsome and charming; indeed, everything a gentleman ought to be. When he was with Jane, he displayed every symptom of a man who is violently in love, but I have heard him boast that whatever he does is done in a hurry. This must certainly explain his repeated ability to separate himself from my sister without taking a proper leave."

"I recall your last letter hinted of Mr. Darcy's rather precipitous leave-taking as well."

"Indeed, he had planned to remain in Hertfordshire longer but he was summoned to Derbyshire by his uncle, the Earl of Matlock. It had to do with the health of his daughter, Lady Victoria Fitzwilliam."

"Pray the young lady's situation is not grave."

"I am afraid that I cannot say. I know this is rather untoward, but I received a letter from Mr. Darcy. I had hoped for some indication of when I might see him again, but the letter provided no such assurance."

"Indeed, it is most unconventional for a single man and a single woman who are not engaged to exchange correspondence. I know how much you admire the young man. Is there something you are at liberty to share about the actual nature of your feelings?"

Elizabeth half smiled and remained silent.

Mrs. Gardiner placed her hand lovingly upon her niece's. "You may keep your secrets. I know that you and Mr. Darcy have been intimate acquaintances for a long time – much longer than the brief span of our relationship – so I dare not council you in that regard. I trust you know what you are about."

The Gardiners stayed a week at Longbourn, and what with the Philipses, the Lucases, and the officers, there was not a day without its engagement. Mrs. Bennet had so carefully provided for the entertainment of her brother and sister that they did not once sit down to a family dinner.

Lady Sophia was much too mindful of the inconvenience her being at Longbourn had caused the Bennet family. Although it would be her first Christmas apart from Elizabeth since they came into each other's lives, she had removed herself to London. Doing so had ensured there would be ample room for the Gardiners to spend Christmas in Hertfordshire, which had long been a family tradition. However, her ladyship did return to Longbourn in January. She immediately detected the gloomy cloud of despair that had fallen over the manor house while she was away. Elizabeth, whose spirits were generally high, seemed pensive and reserved. Jane was nursing a broken heart, and Mrs. Bennet was aggrieved that the heir of the estate, that supercilious Mr. Collins, had chosen to marry Charlotte Lucas.

Lydia was merciless in her teasing of both her older sisters, for, once again, Jane had failed to garner a proposal from the amiable Mr. Bingley, and Elizabeth, with all her wealth and supposed status, had failed to turn the head of the haughty Mr. Darcy. The silly young girl loudly boasted to everyone who would hear that she was certain to be the first Bennet daughter to be married, which pleased her exceedingly, even though it did nothing to heighten her sisters' spirits.

Lady Sophia offered the perfect remedy for everyone's despair. "Why don't all of you join me in town for the Season?"

Mrs. Bennet's pleasure in hearing this was immediate. "Oh, we shall be delighted. What a wonderful thing this will be for my girls."

Indeed, there was but one voice elevated in protest of the scheme — young Lydia's. "Were this any other time, I should be delighted to go to town, for I know London can be quite diverting, but I have more than my share of fun right here in Meryton. Hardly a day goes by that I do not garner the approbation of one officer or another, and I do so adore a man in a red coat."

Mrs. Bennet uncharacteristically admonished her younger daughter. "What nonsense! There shall be many rich gentlemen in town—rich gentlemen, who shall render the officers quite inconsequential."

"Oh, Mama! I would much rather spend my time with the dashing officers in Colonel Forster's regiment. His new wife and I are the dearest of friends. Indeed, she is my closest friend in the world. I should hate to be parted from her."

"For heaven's sake, Lydia, do have some compassion for my nerves. I shall not sacrifice the prospects of all the rest of my daughters just so you might have the pleasure of staying close by your new friend. You are going to town and I will not hear another word to the contrary!"

Persuading Mr. Bennet to accept Lady Sophia's invitation would undoubtedly prove a challenge as well. The one thing he hated more than spending time in town was the notion of doing so in the late duke's home. The prospect of being beholden to such a vile man even if he was dead was abhorrent.

Elizabeth accepted the task of changing her father's mind. Nothing she said, however, seemed to matter. At length, she said, "Papa, how can we heal as a family if you refuse to let go of the past?" Others might try to pass the shame of the late duke's crime onto his daughter-in-law and his grandson and heir all they would, Elizabeth would never be a party to it, and, to the extent that it was within her power, she would not allow others to do so either. "None of what happened in the past was Avery or Lady Sophia's doing, and surely you know they mean the world to me."

"My dearest, Lizzy," he said in response to her plea, "you shall have your Montlake family, which leaves you in the enviable position of having two families, I suppose. I shall never try to persuade you to think meanly of the Montlakes, but they are *your* family — they are not mine. The truth is these people mean nothing at all to me except to serve as my constant reminder of what might have been. Feeling as I do, it is best I do not prevail upon their hospitality. Surely you will agree."

How could she possibly expect Mr. Bennet to be comfortable in the home of the man who had been the means of ruining the best part of his life by depriving him of the chance to see his daughter grow into the beautiful, accomplished woman she had become? He told her as much.

Not to be deterred, Elizabeth said, "Papa, if you will not be prevailed upon to accept Lady Sophia's hospitality, then surely you will consider staying with the Gardiners in Cheapside. Our entire family will be in town. Pray you will oblige me in this one request."

"My dearest Lizzy, I shall ponder the matter."

Chapter 19

At Your Service

Shunning a duke – even one whose family's name was dragged through the mud – was not the thing to do, and thus the doors of the *ton* remained opened to the Montlakes, although the reception at times was not half so warm and inviting as it had been when the late Duke of Dunsmore was alive.

Mr. Bennet had indeed consented to join his family in town. What was more, a glimpse of the library at the Dunsmore Grosvenor Square home gave Mr. Bennet pause to consider that the duke was nothing like his grandfather, after all. If his daughter was determined to have these people be a part of her life, he would not waste another minute of his time on Earth denying her that pleasure purely for the sake of his own injured pride.

Elizabeth, feeling her situation to be fodder for much drawing room drama even still, was content to enjoy the theaters and the occasional ball with those who could be counted as the Montlake family's staunchest advocates. Protecting her sisters' sensibilities was part of it, to be sure. Even Jane, with all her beauty, was deemed merely tolerable among a sea of accomplished debutantes and heiresses awash in large dowries. If Jane garnered so little attention, what chance did Mary and Kitty have? Word that their father was a country gentleman with no wealth to speak of traveled fast.

Still, London could be quite diverting and, all in all, the Bennet sisters had no cause to repine, all except young Lydia who, despite being out in Hertfordshire's rather limited society, was not afforded the same privilege in London, much to Mrs. Bennet's chagrin. She was simply too young and too untamed, and Elizabeth decided, with Lady Sophia's agreement, that if her parents would not take the trouble to protect young Lydia from embarrassing them all, then they would take it upon themselves to limit her ability to do so.

Bingley, being aware that Jane was in town, had indeed begun calling on the Montlakes regularly, which was a balm to Mrs. Bennet's disappointed hopes. It was not long before she started once again speculating aloud of Jane's being the next mistress of Netherfield.

Despite his being Mr. Darcy's friend, Bingley made no mention of Mr. Darcy being in town. Neither did Avery, for that matter, and Elizabeth could only suppose he must still be in Derbyshire.

Egad! The last person in the world whom Elizabeth ever expected to see at the soirée that evening was her odious cousin Mr. Collins. Yet there he was, making a concerted effort navigating the crowded room and heading her way. He was not alone.

Bowing deeply before her, the ridiculous man said, "Cousin Elizabeth, it is my great pleasure to introduce you to my noble patroness, Lady Catherine de Bourgh."

Elizabeth curtsied and expressed her appreciation for the honor her cousin had bestowed, for, indeed, she had been quite eager to make the proud woman's acquaintance for some time. How she wanted to examine the Grande Dame for some resemblance of Mr. Darcy in her countenance and deportment. After her ladyship informed Mr. Collins that his presence was no longer necessary, he quickly ambled away, leaving Elizabeth with the privilege of her ladyship's undivided attention.

Lady Catherine De Bourgh submitted Elizabeth to a thorough inspection before speaking. Her hands resting on her bejeweled walking stick, she said, "So you are Miss Elizabeth Bennet."

"I am, indeed, your ladyship."

She shook her head. "It is a shame the scandal the late Duke of Dunsmore perpetrated against the Bennet family. No doubt it is a subject you would rather not speak on, but I am not in the habit of tempering my speech."

If the grand lady meant to intimidate Elizabeth, she would have no luck. Her true bloodline aside, Elizabeth, too, had been reared steeped in aristocracy. "To know me is to know that I always speak my mind with equal frankness as well, your ladyship. I assure you, Lady Catherine, that my Bennet family is much relieved by the outcome. I am sure you know that we have your own nephew, Mr. Darcy, to thank for unraveling the mystery and leading me back to them."

"I am indeed aware of the role Darcy played in all this, although you cannot be entirely pleased with the outcome of this turn of events."

"I fail to take your meaning, your ladyship."

"Why, you now find yourself being one of five daughters — all in need of husbands. I do not suppose your prospects for forming an advantageous match are nearly as favorable as when you were thought to be the granddaughter of a duke."

Here, Elizabeth merely smiled. How she secretly congratulated herself in being able to boast of her promising prospects with her ladyship's own nephew. *Such knowledge would surely give the old dragon something to contemplate.* "My prospects are as they ever were, I assure you."

"If you insist, although it is a shame that you did not put yourself forward as a possible wife for my parson, Mr. Collins. You might have been the means of assuring your mother's and your sisters' places at the Longbourn estate should some ill fate befall your father."

Elizabeth did not know if she was more aggrieved or relieved by the outcome of that event, but she did not intend to let on any of that to the proud lady. "I am confident my friend Mrs. Collins would argue otherwise."

Her ladyship reared back her head. "I must say, you state your opinion rather decidedly, young woman. Such is a product of your regal upbringing, no doubt. In time, you shall adjust to your reduced circumstances and learn to regard your superiors with all due deference."

"I do not know that I ever shall suppress my own opinions for such a reason as you expound, your ladyship, but I suppose it is generous of you to show such concern for my manner of comportment."

"Pray you are not laughing at me, young woman, when you ought to be thanking me for telling you the things you ought to know if you plan to continue cavorting among Society now that the truth is out. Not everyone will be nearly as generous as I am."

"In such a case as this, your ladyship, I say you must allow me to tend to what is mine while you tend to that which is your own."

With a polite curtsey, Elizabeth walked away. *Oh, the nerve of Lady Catherine de Bourgh — how dare she mention my prospects when she ought to be worrying about her own daughter's? No doubt, she is suffering under the delusion that her daughter is to marry Mr. Darcy.*

A knowing smile graced Elizabeth's countenance over what it would be like to see in her ladyship's face the indignation she would inevitably suffer when Elizabeth was presented to her as her future niece. She had not walked very far when a stranger approached her, although she was certain she saw in his face a resemblance of someone with whom she was particularly familiar.

"I see you have met my aunt."

"Excuse me, sir, but do I know you?"

"No doubt, you know *of* me. Allow me to introduce myself properly. I am Colonel Richard Fitzwilliam at your service." Bowing, he took her proffered hand in his and raised it to his lips.

Elizabeth soon found herself the happy woman seated next to one of the most amiable gentlemen she had met in a long while. Colonel Fitzwilliam entered into conversation directly with the readiness and ease of a well-bred man, and the two of them talked very pleasantly of a great many things. She quickly discerned that a gentleman with his charms rendered even the commonest, dullest, most threadbare topic interesting on those matters he was most eager to discuss. However, on others he had little to say. He did say that his cousin Miss Darcy was in town and residing in her own establishment under the supervision of a Mrs. Annesley.

Elizabeth, having been privy to how all that came to be, gave no indication of how intimate she was with Miss Darcy's story. Further discussion of the Darcys confirmed what she had suspected, that Mr. Darcy was not yet in town. The colonel would not say more, and Elizabeth did not press, supposing it was not her place to do so. If the gentleman had any notion of the nature of Elizabeth's acquaintance with his cousin, he gave no clue.

She could not help but consider that the colonel was nothing at all like his sister, Lady Victoria, who had formed a very unfavorable impression on Elizabeth during all their meetings the Season before. All too soon, Elizabeth was subtly reminded by her companion, Miss Greene, to give some of the others at that evening's gathering their due, and she quitted the colonel's company with but one thought uppermost in her mind.

Colonel Richard Fitzwilliam is one of Mr. Darcy's relations whom I shall enjoy knowing very much.

Chapter 20

A Pleasant Trip

Less than a week later, Elizabeth espied Darcy at the theater. She did not know at first whether to be glad about his being in town or troubled that he was in London and had not made that fact known to her. There he sat in the Matlocks' luxury box, dressed in stark black and white and looking incredibly handsome. Sitting in front of him was his cousin Lady Victoria.

Elizabeth arched her brow. *It appears the young woman has undergone a complete recovery from whatever mysterious affliction ailed her.*

She silently questioned what Mr. Darcy was about. How long had he been in town and why the secrecy, for had the colonel not informed her that he did not know when Darcy would arrive in town for the Season? She could hardly wait until the intermezzo so she might speak with him, and, rather than pay attention to the performance on stage, she soon began plotting the means for putting herself directly in his path.

When at last she and Darcy stood directly before each other, his face showed a mixture of disquiet and surprise, and his demeanor was rather unreadable. *Is he glad to see me?*

After a neat bow from him and a curtsey from her, Elizabeth said, "Mr. Darcy, I did not expect to see you of all people this evening. I thought you were in Derbyshire. When did you arrive in town?"

"No, I'm here. I arrived this morning. I did not expect to see you here either."

"Oh? Is this not one of the most highly anticipated events of the Season? Where else would I be?"

"No—of course you are here. What I meant to say is I had planned to call on you tomorrow."

"At least there is that."

"I beg your pardon?"

"Sir, if you only arrived this morning, as you say you did, and I have no reason to doubt your word, I am surprised at your even being here. One would have thought you would be weary from your travels." A barely perceptible nod of his head was encouragement enough for Elizabeth to continue. "I trust you had a pleasant trip."

"I did — thank you. Coming here tonight was not my idea. My cousin — "

Before Darcy could complete his sentence, he and Elizabeth were joined by a third party — his cousin Lady Victoria.

She laced her arm through his. "Here you are, my dearest cousin." She looked at Elizabeth. Feigning surprise, she said, "Ah, I beg your pardon, but what shall I call you? Is it Lady Elizabeth? Miss Bennet, perhaps?"

Elizabeth noticed Darcy stiffen in the face of his cousin's brashness. *And how dare she assume such a cozy relationship with the gentleman, even if they are cousins. Unless —*

"You may call me by my name — Miss Elizabeth Bennet."

"How very formal," said the other woman. She pursed her lips. "And here I always supposed you and I were such *intimate* friends." She made a show of clinging more tightly to Mr. Darcy's arm. "You won't mind if I steal my handsome cousin away, I'm sure. You must come with me, my dear, for one of my oldest friends is here, and she is impatient to wish us joy — "

Darcy interrupted, "Lady Victoria!"

"What did I say?" she cried, as she started walking away, forcefully pulling him along.

Darcy looked back at Elizabeth, his eyes filled with unspoken apology, leaving her to wonder what had just happened. An enormous lump formed in her throat. Her heart slammed against her chest. *Why would anyone be wishing Mr. Darcy and his cousin joy?*

Very early the following day, Lady Catherine stormed into Matlock House demanding to see her brother, the earl, at once. She insisted upon knowing the meaning of the rumors making their way through the *ton* that Darcy was to marry the earl's daughter, Lady Victoria.

"Calm yourself, Catherine. You know as well as anyone how close those two have always been. It should not come as a surprise to you that their friendship has blossomed into something more meaningful and lasting."

"This is not to be borne. Why, it was the favorite wish of our sister, Anne, as well as my own, that Darcy was destined to marry my daughter, our dear sister's own namesake. I will not have my own hopes and dreams thwarted by the whims of your selfish daughter, who has always considered herself superior to my Anne."

"I am afraid it is beyond your power to do anything to prevent this union."

"Nonsense! I am not in the habit of brokering disappointment. I will do everything in my power to see an end to this madness."

"And I will do everything in my power to see that the union takes place. My family's honor is at stake."

"Pray what is that supposed to mean?"

"What I am saying, Catherine" — here the earl arose from his chair — "and I trust you will keep this to yourself... Victoria is with child."

Her ladyship's amazement was evident. "There must be some mistake. I refuse to believe it. I will speak to my nephew at once to find out the truth."

"You are free to speak with Darcy all you like, and, while you're at it, pray prevail upon him to act swiftly before society becomes aware of Victoria's situation. I swear if he were anyone else, I would be obliged to call him out. I am not at all certain it may not come to that."

"So you mean to say that Darcy does not intend to marry her? If that is the case, he must doubt the truthfulness of her claim."

"Sadly, the situation has proved to be the means of a great divide with Darcy, for he has assured me that he will require more than my daughter's word on the matter. He requires proof that only the passage of time will afford."

"That you would abide such a scheme is evidence enough that you, too, harbor doubts."

"I know our nephew to be a decent, honorable man. He vows that nothing that might be considered untoward happened between him and Victoria. She insists otherwise. Indeed, it is a matter of his word against hers. Only time will tell."

Not Wholly Unfounded

Darcy received an early morning summons from Avery to meet him at White's. He hated it when his friend asserted his ducal airs, but the fact of the matter was that Avery was indeed a duke, and one did not deny a duke a command appearance.

To make matters worse, Avery was late. Sitting at the table, awaiting His Grace's arrival, gave Darcy time to remember his having to wait for Avery another time. It was the first time he could ever recall having been alone with Elizabeth. Darcy recalled her teasing manner and how she would not be satisfied until she had captured his full attention. Even then he knew he was in danger of one day losing his heart to her—Lady Elizabeth Montlake, the younger sister of one of his closest friends.

Darcy wondered how close he and Avery would be after that morning. *Can our friendship survive yet another test?*

The initial test had been when Darcy brought the late Duke of Dunsmore's crime to light. Family loyalty had insisted that Avery balk at the notion that his grandfather had committed such a heinous act as rob another family of their child and pass her off as his own son's illegitimate daughter. Only the threat of blackmail from one of the late duke's former associates had persuaded Avery of the veracity of Darcy's claims. Thus persuaded, Darcy and Avery joined forces in reuniting Elizabeth with the Bennets.

When, at last, Avery arrived, he came straight to the point of his being there. "You can have no doubt why I asked you to see me here this morning, Darcy, away from my home."

"I would imagine it has to do with my presence at the theater last night."

"Where you go matters not in the least to me. I am more concerned about who you were seen with at the theater."

"Look, Avery, I won't play games with you. No doubt you've heard about my situation with my cousin Lady Victoria by now. You ought to know that, despite what it looks like, this matter is riddled with complications."

"The only thing I need to know is whether the rumor that you and Lady Victoria are to be married is true."

"I am afraid that the rumor is not wholly un-founded."

"Then you do not deny it?"

"As I said, it's complicated." Darcy then proceeded to discuss the intricacies of his situation with his cousin that he felt at liberty to share with Avery.

Little difference did any of what Darcy said make to the duke. "No one can be surprised by this development, Darcy. Look at how you and your cousin have comported yourselves over the years. Now you speak of loving her. If that is the case, then what does it matter if she is lying or not? There appears to be more than enough affection on her part for both of you.

"I do not need to tell you how disappointed I am, owing to what this means to my sister. I am not unaware that the two of you have an understanding, nor do I fault you. To do so would render me a hypocrite in light of my own behavior towards Miss Hamilton."

"I am glad you understand."

"What I understand is that my sister will be devastated by this development. I am aware that you only arrived in town yesterday, which must be your excuse for not informing Elizabeth that you are encumbered. I expect you to tell her today."

Elizabeth's busy mind did not know what to make of what was happening. Mr. Darcy had not called on her as promised, leaving her with little choice other than to conjecture the meaning of his cousin's words the evening before on her own. Wanting to escape the confines of the house in order to dwell on those matters that must surely exasperate her, Elizabeth grabbed her wrap and headed outside. Ever vigilant, Miss Greene soon followed.

Elizabeth had not walked very far when, to her surprise, she espied Mr. Darcy straight ahead. No doubt, he meant to call on her at her home. She considered it quite fortunate that they would spend time together, just the two of them, without exciting her mama's hopes that he might actually be calling on her sister Kitty. Turning to her companion, Elizabeth asked for time alone with Mr. Darcy.

"I shall allow a discrete distance between us, but His Grace would object were I to abandon you altogether," said Miss Greene.

"Yes, and we both know that what His Grace wants His Grace gets, do we not?"

"I am merely doing my job, my lady."

"Pray, forgive my shortness, Miss Greene." By now, Darcy and Elizabeth were mere steps apart. Nodding to her companion as a means of tacitly commanding her to stay right where she was, Elizabeth walked to where Darcy stood.

He bowed and she curtsied. Darcy said, "I was on my way to see you. Are you expected elsewhere?"

"No, sir, I simply wanted time away from the house — to take in the fresh air."

"May I walk with you?"

"I do not know that I can stop you, sir, if that is your desire."

"You're angry with me. I am sure I know the reason. There is much for us to discuss," he said, falling in step beside her. "Allow me to start by apologizing for my cousin's unseemly behavior last evening at the theater."

"You surprise me, sir. You have never taken it upon yourself to apologize for your cousin's rudeness before. Why are you doing so now? Or does the fact that others are wishing the two of you joy oblige you to speak for her?"

"It was wrong of Lady Victoria to insinuate that our situation called for such felicitations. She meant to rattle you with premature suppositions."

"Premature suppositions? Speak plainly, Mr. Darcy."

Darcy commenced telling Elizabeth everything that he had told Avery earlier but in terms more suitable to her maidenly sensibilities. Throughout his speech, Elizabeth colored, she fumed, and she silently questioned.

Does he honestly expect me to believe that he is being falsely accused of fathering a child? That his cousin's claims cannot possibly be true, because he has no remembrance of any such transgression? Does he suppose I am completely naïve?

"My stance is that my cousin's duplicity will soon become known. Patience and a sufficient passage of time is all this situation requires."

Elizabeth could not believe she was hearing him correctly. She said nothing.

As if taking Elizabeth's silence as encouragement to push forth the merits of his proposal, Mr. Darcy pressed on. "Elizabeth, you asked me to wait for you, and I did. Is it too much for me to ask that you wait for me?"

"How dare you compare the two situations? I asked for time to reunite with my family, not wait to see if a child is the consequence of a union that you will not even acknowledge."

Searching her face for a modicum of understanding and finding none, he persisted. "I cannot acknowledge that of which I have no remembrance."

"What does that even mean, Mr. Darcy? Either the two of you shared intimacies that ought to be reserved for a husband and wife or – heaven forbid – a man and his mistress, or you did not."

He swept his fingers through his hair. "She cared for me when I was recovering from the injuries I sustained in the carriage accident. I was in and out of consciousness. Those weeks are lost to me, but I am sure that, had I engaged in such intimacies as she suggests occurred, I would remember."

"And if a child is born then what do you plan to do, sir?"

"I am obligated to marry her."

"But what if the child is not yours?"

"Then I am obliged to save her."

Elizabeth was unable to hide the pain in her voice. "You love her?"

"No — no, not in the way you mean. I love you. I have always loved you. I always will love you — only you. I want to spend my life with you."

"Then how exactly do you feel about her?"

"I … I love her as a cousin ought to love a cousin."

Elizabeth's heartbeat thundered with rage. Her temper she dared not vouch for. "If you love her, then for heaven's sake, go … be with her. Many a marriage has survived with less affection than you profess towards your cousin. As much as she loves you, no doubt she will be everything you would wish for in a wife."

He shook his head. "You're wrong. You are everything I wish for in a wife."

"Were that the case then you would not be doing this."

"Would that it were only that simple."

"As I do not quite see the complication that you continue alluding to, I do not see that there's any point in further discussion. Take this — " she struggled, but managed to rip the gold necklace from her neck, sending the single white pearl flying through the air " — and take your broken promises and pray leave me alone, Mr. Darcy!"

Her severe reaction coupled with her biting tone pierced him deeply. No doubt, she was in pain. He was in pain too. This situation was agonizing for both of them. Surmising hers was greater than his due to its suddenness, he reached out his hand to her, not to accept the necklace, but to comfort her. "Elizabeth, my love?"

She recoiled from his touch. "Do not refer to me in such endearing terms! I never wish to hear you speak to me in such a manner ever again. Goodbye, Mr. Darcy."

With those words, she hastily turned and set off in Miss Greene's direction. The turmoil in Elizabeth's mind was now painfully great. She quickly outpaced her companion, still clutching the broken chain he had refused to accept. She had trusted this man, depended upon him, loved him.

How dare he betray me in such a manner as this? I shall never forgive him!

Chapter 22

Utterly Uncontrolled

All the gloom of Lydia's attitude was cleared away when she received a letter from her particular friend, Mrs. Harriet Forster, the wife of the regiment encamped outside of Meryton. The letter was but a single sheet and covered with words scratched across every possible inch of the page. It spoke of Harriet's boredom now that Lydia was in London. She would like nothing better than for Lydia to be her particular guest when the militia set up camp in Brighton.

Lydia's enthusiasm on this occasion was scarcely to be contained.

"Oh, Mama, may I please, please go to Brighton with my friend?"

"I do not know that that is such a wise idea. Besides, your prospects of finding a rich husband are much brighter here in town."

"But, Mama, how am I to meet anyone when I am not even allowed to attend any of the elegant balls? I am sure I will find Brighton far more diverting. Besides, that is where all the officers will be: Mr. Wickham, Mr. Denny."

"Oh, Lydia. It is so unfair that Lizzy will not allow you to accompany her to the balls along with Jane, Mary, and Kitty, but I do not know that it will be fair to deny the older girls their share of fun here in town by cutting their visit short."

"Whatever do you mean? My sisters are not invited to come."

"Surely you do not suppose I will allow you to travel to Brighton without a mother's supervision? Why, I must remain here with your sisters to see that they are making the most of their time in town to find rich husbands."

"In traveling to Brighton as my friend Harriet's guest, I am certain to be well supervised, for she is a married woman and her husband is the colonel. What better assurance do you need that I will be well looked after?"

Mrs. Bennet placed her finger on her chin. "I suppose you have a point. Indeed, it sounds like a very agreeable scheme. I know that, were I able to travel to Brighton, I most certainly would. A little sea-bathing would set me up forever, but first you must speak with your father to obtain his permission."

With that bit of encouragement, Lydia happily skipped off. Of course her father would say yes. When had he ever given himself the trouble of answering no to any of her petitions? She was mightily tempted to turn a somersault mid-stride, and she would have if she had been out of doors. "I'm going to Brighton," she said, her voice a merry tune. "I'm going to Brighton."

Elizabeth was not equal to the task of facing anyone after seeing Mr. Darcy—not her sister Jane, not Avery, who would be annoyed that she and Darcy even had a secret understanding in the first place, and not Lady Sophia, who would know better than anyone would how wounded Elizabeth was as a result of this disheartening change of fortune. She certainly did not want to be bothered with her mama's foolishness about finding husbands for her daughters at such a time as this. She did not have to, for, immediately upon entering the house, she discerned that the urgency of Lydia's situation outweighed her own distress.

Elizabeth was all too aware that young Lydia was not happy about being away from Meryton. Indeed, she had gone from being everybody's darling in the confines of Meryton to rather insignificant in London. Not only was she not so rich as the other young ladies, her wild behavior, whenever she was allowed to have fun with her sisters, made her more of a spectacle than an object of admiration among the gentlemen who sought women with either fortune, connection, or both, as prospective brides.

All that would change were she to travel with the Forsters to Brighton, for she had always been a favorite of the officers — they noticed her and made her feel special. In Lydia's imagination, a visit to Brighton comprised every possibility of earthly happiness. She saw, with the creative eye of fancy, the streets of that gay bathing-place covered with officers. She saw all the glories of the camp — its tents stretched forth in beauteous uniformity of lines, crowded with the young and the gay, and dazzling with scarlet. To complete the view, she saw herself seated beneath a tent, tenderly flirting with at least six officers at once. A season in London that confined her to the occasional exhibition or play was nothing by comparison.

Vain, ignorant, and utterly uncontrolled, Lydia wants only encouragement to make herself an embarrassment to us all. If ever there was a time when her sister needed reigning in, this was it. Elizabeth knew that she would have to be the one to prevail upon her father to deny Lydia such opportunity.

Mr. Bennet listened to Elizabeth attentively and seeing she was so passionate and her plea so ardent, he affectionately took her by the hand. "Do not make yourself uneasy, my love. I fail to see the harm in allowing her to go. She has been miserable since coming to town, and, as you well know, when Lydia is miserable the entire household is miserable, for she will not have it any other way."

"But, Papa, a young girl with Lydia's exuberant spirits will surely find herself in trouble with so much temptation, and so little supervision, and absolutely no parental guidance."

"I trust the colonel and his wife will see that she comes to no harm."

"With all due respect, the colonel will be busy with his own affairs, and his wife is scarcely more than a child herself."

"I am afraid the decision is made. Lydia will go to Brighton, and I shall enjoy a peaceful reprieve while she is gone."

"Is that all you ever think about?"

He reared back his head. "I beg your pardon, young lady?"

"Sir, you speak of Lydia's going away as the difference between you enjoying peace versus turmoil — as though that is all that is at stake, when really it has nothing at all to do with your comfort and everything to do with your daughter's safety and your family's reputation."

Letting go of Elizabeth's hand, Mr. Bennet steeled his expression. "I will not be told how I shall and shall not behave as regards my family's safety or even my family's reputation, not by you—not by anyone. Do you understand me? No one knows how I have suffered. How I decide to bear my lot in life is no one's concern but my own."

"It is a father's job to protect his family, not ridicule them and send them away when they do not meet with his pleasure."

"How do you know what a father should and should not do when your greatest example in that regard was a detestable child abductor whom you foolishly consider as someone worthy of esteem de-spite all the prevailing wisdom to the contrary?"

Elizabeth recoiled at the cold hearted and hurt-ful manner of his reproach. When would he see that she would never allow herself to learn to hate the late duke, despite what he had done? The man who had committed those unspeakable crimes was not the man she remembered — the man whom she had adored for the better part of her life.

If only her papa had it in him, if not to forgive, then surely to show some understanding and compas-sion. She would not entertain that discussion with him again—not in that moment. Disappointed and sorry, yet forced to be content that she had done her part in protecting her sister, she left him to his book. She did not intend to increase her vexations by dwelling on them. She was confident of having performed her duty, and there was nothing more to do.

Besides, there was the matter of her painful parting of ways with Mr. Darcy. A part of her insisted that no good would come from dwelling on what might have been, even though her heart whispered it would be a long time before she would understand or forgive him for what he had done.

Chapter 23

So Far Away

Avery sought out Elizabeth later that evening to determine how she had left things with his friend. "I spoke with Darcy this morning at the club."

"Then you know that he and his cousin—"

Avery interrupted Elizabeth. "I know that he has wounded you deeply and, depending upon how things unfold, I do not know that I will ever forgive him."

"You knew?"

"I'm not blind, Elizabeth."

"I feel like such a fool."

"You have no reason to feel that way. You did nothing wrong. You followed your heart. Things do not always unfold as we plan. I, too, have had to examine the workings of my heart because of all this. I am afraid you and mother will not be pleased with what I am about to tell you."

"What is it, Avery?"

"You see, in my haste to chastise Darcy for his ill-treatment toward you, I realized that I have behaved just as poorly with the woman I love. This afternoon, I made amends for my inattentiveness. I offered Miss Hamilton my hand in marriage, and she accepted. Margaret is to be the next Duchess of Dunsmore."

Elizabeth's stunned silence encouraged Avery to continue. "You have nothing to say? I know you never liked her, but I expect you to pretend to be happy for me."

"Indeed, I wish you great joy, Avery."

"Your tone insists otherwise, dear Sister, but I suppose you will come around in time."

"Yes, in time. I suppose we shall be privy to a fair degree of her company now that you are officially engaged."

"Indeed. Her family will dine with us early next week. By then I am confident our mother will have accustomed herself to the fact that the next

Duchess of Dunsmore does not descend from noble lineage."

Endeavoring to lighten the atmosphere for Avery's sake, Elizabeth said, "Oh dear! That reminds me of something."

"What, pray tell?"

"You listed the members of our family who will not be pleased to hear of your engagement, but you neglected to mention my mama. You have not the slightest notion of what the loss of yet another potential son-in-law will do to her poor nerves."

"I know what you're doing, Elizabeth. You are trying to hide your pain for the sake of my joy. If I have one regret with the timing of all this, it is that it coincides with your heartbreak."

"I'm certain that, in time, any anguish I'm now suffering will fade." Again, her voice filled with optimism that she did not feel. "Besides, I've heard it said that the endings of all things are but the beginnings of other, more beautiful things to come. It is only fitting that you should know the joy you are no doubt feeling. You've certainly waited long enough."

"I did not mean for my joy to overshadow the heartache you must be feeling. I know how much you esteem Darcy and, likewise, how deeply he cares for you."

"Indeed. He promised he would wait for me." She shrugged. "So much for promises."

Avery took Elizabeth by the hand. "I do not know what Darcy told you, but he has assured me that this situation is not of his choosing."

"I cannot agree. One always has a choice. He chose his cousin."

"You know that, as much as I do not want this, I have asked Darcy to stay away. Trust me, it is better this way. Darcy is an honorable man, but until this matter is resolved one way or another, it is better that he keeps his distance from you."

Elizabeth and Darcy had not crossed paths in weeks. As she did not intend to shrink from society and, in so doing, add to her misery, she went about the business of enjoying all the Season's gaieties. She surmised that he was the one eschewing society. It was just as well, for the last thing she wanted or needed to see was Mr. Darcy parading about with his cousin Lady Victoria.

Elizabeth may not have seen Darcy, but that was not to say he had not seen her. On one particular evening, Darcy stood on the balcony overlooking a crowded ballroom floor. He had but one purpose in mind, that being to gaze upon her from a discrete distance. He saw her standing there with her sisters Miss Bennet and Miss Mary by her side. How lovely she looked. He was certain that he could stand there and gaze upon her all night. He longed for the right to go to her and request a set. His blindness to his cousin's faults had stripped him of that privilege. He silently chastised himself, for he had no one to blame but himself. *We are so close, yet so far away.*

Elizabeth's wandering eyes afforded her a glimpse of Darcy standing there, so close, yet so far away. Her wounded heart told her to look elsewhere lest their eyes meet. It would not do. He was scanning the crowd below. Was he looking for her? *Even if he is, what does it matter? He made his choice.*

Gazing up at him and yet pretending to do otherwise, Elizabeth silently berated herself. How dare her foolish heart yearn for him? How dare her lips long for the lingering touch of his? How dare her body scream for the comfort of his tender embrace? If only she had not allowed him a lover's prerogative then she would not know what she was missing.

A cautioning voice once again urged her to look away before he noticed her. A moment later proved too late. Their eyes met.

Imagine You There

Too many words unspoken stood between them. Their eyes holding fast upon each other's, his silent beckoning would have to be enough.

My dearest, loveliest Elizabeth, I long for you. It is all I can do not to think of you. Whenever I close my eyes, I imagine you there. When I dream, I dream only of you. Harsh reality then awakens me, and I find that you and I are yet so far away from each other. How I long to stand before you and tell you that this nightmare has come to an end.

A familiar voice abruptly recalled him to his surroundings. "What are you doing, Darcy?"

Darcy turned to face the younger man. "Am I to answer to you, Your Grace?"

"When it comes to my sister's well-being — most certainly!"

Darcy returned his gaze to where Elizabeth was standing. Silent questions showed in her eyes.

"Do you not consider that she deserves more than false promises and disappointed hopes? I am afraid that is the only thing you're in the position to offer."

"You know I only want what is best for her."

"If that is the case, then abide by your promise to stay away from her."

Parting as amiably as the situation allowed, the two men went their separate ways. Darcy realized too late that he had put himself directly in Miss Caroline Bingley's path. She immediately seized upon him.

"Mr. Darcy, where have you been keeping yourself? I dare say it's been weeks since I last saw you."

"How are you getting along, Miss Bingley?"

"Why, I have to say things are much better now."

Darcy, wanting to be on his way, said nothing.

His silence only encouraged her. "I would ask if the rumors that have been quietly circulating all about of your imminent betrothal to Lady Victoria Fitzwilliam had any basis, but seeing that you are here and not basking in Eliza Bennet's fine eyes, I can only assume that what I've been hearing is true. You must certainly consider yourself most fortunate to have escaped the possibility of an alliance with such a family."

"What do you want, Miss Bingley?"

"Why, I wish to congratulate you, of course. No one of your standing should have to suffer such degradation."

"I believe you and I have ventured down this road before."

"I take it you are referring to my brother."

Indeed he was. Bingley and Miss Bennet were standing with Elizabeth even as Darcy and Miss Bingley were speaking. How Darcy wished he were at liberty to join them, but the situation prohibited it. The last thing he wanted to do was cause Elizabeth more pain than he had already inflicted upon her.

"Your brother appears to be as enamored of Miss Bennet as ever before."

"That may be, but I detect no greater symptom of love in Miss Bennet for my brother than when we were last in Hertfordshire. No doubt Charles is of the same mind. You and I both know my brother well enough to know that once someone is out of his sight, the poor soul is as good as out of his mind. Those awful Bennets will not remain in town much longer, I'm certain. Soon my brother's heart will be fixed upon another young woman with an angelic countenance."

Later on, Avery sought out Elizabeth, who had left her sister's side. He was concerned that she might have been unsettled by Darcy's presence. Indeed she was, for he found her standing outside, all by herself, looking sad and lonely.

"Elizabeth, how are you getting along this evening?"

"I wish you would not worry about me. I shall be quite all right."

"It is my duty to worry about you. I know you are aware that Darcy is here. I saw the two of you looking at each other."

There was no point in denying it. She missed Mr. Darcy exceedingly. Even before they were lovers, they had been friends. For the longest time, when her world seemed to be spinning out of control, she only needed to think of him. To know she could no longer rely upon his steadfastness was unbearable.

"Avery, pray tell me how is this to be endured?" She had meant to be strong, for it was not in her nature to dwell on matters that would only serve to cause her pain. When Avery took her into his arms, she openly wept.

"Elizabeth, my dear, let me take you home."

Chapter 25

Hope for a Future

Around twelve at night, just as everyone had gone to bed, an express came from Colonel Forster informing Mr. Bennet that his youngest daughter had run off with one of the officers – to own the truth – Mr. Wickham! What a surprise this was and one that created quite a stir. Frantic hours later, Mr. Bennet found himself across town in Cheapside, sitting in Mr. Gardiner's study. After explaining all that had happened as spelled out in the colonel's correspondence, he handed his brother the letter that Lydia had meant for her friend Mrs. Forster's eyes only. The colonel had seen fit to include it in his express.

Mr. Gardiner read the missive in silence.

My Dear Harriette,

You will laugh when you know where I am gone, and I cannot help laughing myself at your surprise to-morrow morning, as soon as I am missed. I am going to Gretna Green, and if you cannot guess with whom, I shall think you a simpleton, for there is but one man in the world I love, and he is an angel. I should never be happy without him, so think it no harm to be off. You need not send word to my parents of my going, if you do not like, for it will make the surprise the greater when I write to them and sign my name "Lydia Wickham." What a good joke it will be! I can hardly write for laughing. Pray make my excuses to Pratt for not keeping my engagement, and dancing with him tonight. Tell him I hope he will excuse me when he knows all, and tell him I will dance with him at the next ball we meet, with great pleasure. I shall send for my clothes when I get to Longbourn, but I wish you would tell Sally to mend a great slit in my muslin gown before they are packed up. Good-bye. Give my love to Colonel Forster. I hope you will drink to our good journey.

Your affectionate friend,

Lydia Bennet

It was all Mr. Gardiner could do to resist balling up the paper and tossing it into the fireplace. "That foolish girl," he said.

Mr. Bennet said, "Were it only the case that the two of them are indeed on their way to Gretna Green. As unfortunate as such an alliance would be, it is far better than the alternative. But I do not have the slightest hope."

"Please be assured, Brother, I will do all in my power to assist you in bringing about a better outcome than the current situation foretells."

"That's why I have come to you. I had hoped you would offer your assistance. To be honest, the Duke of Dunsmore offered to be of service as well. I was loathe to accept his benevolence, but my Lizzy insisted that I do."

"You were wise to set aside your pride. We need all the help we can muster."

Mr. Thomas Bennet suffered feelings akin to having failed his family completely. He should never have agreed to Lydia's going away with the Forsters, but he supposed he would have no peace otherwise. Now he decided it was best to remove his family from London owing to the scandal.

"You ought to know that my family is preparing to return to Longbourn as we speak. In light of the scandal, it is best for all concerned, especially Mrs. Bennet who is beside herself with grief."

"Do you mean to impose this scheme upon all of your daughters including Jane and Elizabeth?" said Mr. Gardiner.

Mr. Bennet said, "Jane being the eldest, no doubt, knows her place. However, as regards my next eldest, I am afraid our dear Lizzy has lived above her true self for so very long that she may never be truly happy living the sort of life that our circumstances will allow. Add to that, she tried her best to caution me against allowing Lydia to travel to Brighton. She felt strongly that something like this would happen. I fear this travesty may be the means of our losing her all over again, should she choose to remain here in town with the Montlakes."

Lydia's misadventures would no doubt cause every upstanding person in London to turn against the Bennet family. Elizabeth did not intend to be one of them. As for her disappointment with her father, she resolved that now was not the time for recriminations. Recovering Lydia would not be easy. Her papa needed all the love and support he could get in seeing his family through the crisis.

Lady Sophia walked into Elizabeth's apartment. Seeing the maids packing her trunks was particularly alarming. "Elizabeth, what in heavens is going on? Why are you packing?"

"Papa left word before heading to Gracechurch Street that he means for the entire family to return to Longbourn post haste in the wake of Lydia's scandalous behavior."

Avery, having heard from a servant that all the Bennets were preparing for a precipitous return to Longbourn, strolled into Elizabeth's room in time to hear her speech. Both he and Lady Sophia argued that Elizabeth need not leave because of the Bennet family's shame. It seemed their arguments were in vain.

Elizabeth said, "Oh, but you see I honestly believe I must."

"Why tie yourself to the Bennets' lot?" Lady Sophia cried.

"I am a Bennet!"

Avery took Elizabeth by her hand and persuaded her to cease her packing and sit next to him. "True, you are indeed a Bennet. However, you are my sister. I cannot imagine you not being a part of one of the most important days of my life or have you failed to remember that the eve of my wedding is fast approaching?"

Elizabeth felt a tinge of mortification spread all over her body. "Dearest Avery, pray forgive me for thinking only of myself. However, the shame of what Lydia has done will inevitably affect you as well. Is it not better that I take my leave of London with the rest of my Bennet family and along with it the disgrace?"

"Elizabeth, do you forget with whom you are speaking? I am the Duke of Dunsmore. I could parade through the streets of London in nothing but a cloth sack and it would not diminish my standing in the eyes of society. Pray you will remain here in town with mother and me, at least until the wedding. Then, if you must return to Longbourn, you may. In fact, why don't you speak with Miss Bennet and invite her to stay as well? I know how you depend on her."

After agreeing to Avery's request, Elizabeth soon found herself in Jane's room. Persuading Jane to stay in town was not as easy as Elizabeth had hoped.

"What about Mr. Bingley, dearest Jane?"

"What about him, Lizzy?"

Elizabeth placed her hand on her sister's. "Pray you have not abandoned hope for a future with him."

"Please do not misunderstand me. While I am sure there is someone somewhere for me, I am not convinced it's Mr. Bingley."

"Jane?"

"I am quite all right with it, believe me, Lizzy. I believe I have come to embrace a bit of your sentimentality in that regard in that I do not intend to make myself upset over things best not to be dwelt upon."

"You have waited so long —"

Jane interrupted. "One might say I have waited too long. How many opportunities have we had to get it right? First, there was his coming to Hertfordshire and letting the Netherfield estate. Then there was Pemberley. Both of those times, he left with not even a goodbye. The same must be said of the last time we were all together in Hertfordshire."

The more Elizabeth listened to her sister expound the reasons she was convinced that the whole of the acquaintance with Mr. Bingley was little more than a fond attraction on his part that only manifested when they were in company, the more she was convinced that Jane's reasoning was sound. Theirs was an acquaintance not of many years like that of Elizabeth and Mr. Darcy's, but rather two months or so, spread out over the course of two years. If Elizabeth and Mr. Darcy's relationship was not meant to be, it was equally likely that neither was Jane and Mr. Bingley's.

Be that as it may, Elizabeth felt it was insufficient cause for Jane not to remain in town. "Jane, won't you reconsider?"

"Oh, Lizzy, I would love to stay here in town with you, but you've seen how my mother is taking the news. My place is at Longbourn with the rest of the family." Thinking she may have wounded her sister, Jane said, "Lizzy, it is only right that you stay here in town to be a part of His Grace's wedding celebration. No doubt he and Lady Sophia are depending upon you. You and I are family and nothing will ever change that, but the same must be said of you and the Montlakes. They also are your family. However, Lizzy – and pray do not think me insensitive – but they are not mine. I do not belong here. I belong at Longbourn."

Chapter 26

Proof Enough

Darcy had been out of town for a week, which gave him a much-needed reprieve from his 'obligation' to pay daily visits to his family at Matlock House. He and Lady Victoria always had bent the rules of proper decorum by spending time solely in each other's company, yet it vexed him that his uncle and aunt, Lord and Lady Matlock, afforded them that same freedom now. The last thing he wanted was time alone with his cousin.

Their time together of late was not nearly as pleasant as it had been before their circumstances changed. She was more than a little upset that, not only had he refused to consent to a wedding date, he had not even made her a formal declaration of marriage. Once again, he reminded her of his reason.

"I thought I made it clear to you that I do not believe anything untoward happened between us. Hence, I will not marry you until I am convinced that you are with child, even if that means that we marry on the eve of the supposed child's birth." In truth, his honor dictated that he marry her sooner than that, but angry people did not always behave as dictated by honor.

"How can you be so cruel?" She impudently placed her hand on her increasing waistline." Is this not proof enough?"

Darcy huffed. "It proves nothing, other than my suspicion that you ought to push away from the table sooner."

Aggrieved and offended, her ladyship picked up a porcelain knickknack from a nearby table and hurled it at him. Darcy ducked his head just in time to avoid the whizzing weapon. Rather than chastise her, he merely ignored her, which only increased her ire.

Standing, Lady Victoria meant to cross the room to demand that he pay her the proper consideration she thought she deserved, but in her haste she tripped and fell. Her head landed against the sharp end of the table and thus rendered her unconscious.

Seeing this, Darcy was horrified. He raced to her and dropped down on his knees. "Victoria," he said while attempting to revive and comfort her. In rushed a footman who must have heard the commotion. Darcy yelled, "Her ladyship is in need of medical attention. Hurry!"

Some hours later, Darcy wore a path in the carpet as he paced the floor, consumed with worry. At least her ladyship had regained consciousness, but he had no way of knowing whether there was any lasting damage because of her fall. Espying the physician descending the stairs, he rushed to him, wanting to know if his cousin was capable of receiving company.

"Her parents are with her now."

"Mr. West, you have been our family physician for years. I have a matter I wish to discuss with you that may seem a bit untoward, but it is vital that I know the truth."

"What is it that you wish to know?"

"I need to know about the unborn child."

"I beg your pardon, sir? What unborn child?"

"Lady Victoria—"

"—Mr. Darcy, I can safely say there is nothing to be concerned with in that regard."

Darcy felt himself growing pale. "Are you saying that the child—the accident?"

"I am afraid that what I am saying, sir, is there is no reason for us to be having this discussion, for there would be nothing to discuss ... not now and certainly not before."

As angry and disgusted as he was, Darcy did not confront his cousin with malice, but rather with cool civility. He regarded her as though she was no more than a stranger to him. Lady Victoria, having suffered a mild concussion, sat in a comfortable chair overlooking the garden.

Standing in the doorway of his cousin's apartment, waiting for her maid to finish what she was doing and then leave the room, Darcy recalled a pact he had made with his cousin when they were children that they would always be the best of friends. They had even pricked their fingers and sealed their avowal in blood. He shook his head. *What happened to her?*

When the maid quit the room, Darcy said, "I have spoken to the physician. You lied to me — just as I suspected. Now, tell me what really happened — were you violated? Did I behave in an ungentlemanly manner towards you?"

Her head bandaged, her ladyship looked at Darcy unapologetically. "If indeed anything did happen between us, I would not consider it a violation but rather an affirmation of our love."

"You are hell-bent on omitting one crucial fact, Victoria. I do not love you — not in the manner you suggest."

"But I love you and, given that your chances with *her* are ruined, why should you not love me?"

"Pray answer the question, did we or did we not?"

She exhaled a frustrated breath. "No, we did not—not actually, but I spent more than one night in your bed, which must be the same thing in the eyes of the world."

Darcy's mouth gaped. He colored, but he would not be silent. "I beg to differ! I will not relinquish my own hopes and dreams because of your selfish recklessness. You have no one to blame but yourself for your own actions. Any damage to your reputation as a consequence of your duplicity is indeed your misfortune."

"I know what I did was wrong, but how dare you speak to me so callously? What's more, how dare you look at me as though you despise me?"

Darcy, by now, had taken a seat in the opposite corner of the room. "You cost me the woman I love."

Lady Victoria disdainfully cast her eyes towards the ceiling. "You ought to be thanking me for sparing you the shame of being connected with such a family."

Darcy stood. "I will not hear another word spoken against the Bennets, not from you. Not after what you've done."

Her ladyship gave her cousin a dismissive huff. "What I did is nothing in comparison to the youngest Bennet daughter who is known to be living in sin with your adversary — George Wickham."

He sucked in a sharp breath. "You do not know what you are talking about."

"If you don't believe me, ask my brother Richard. He is the one who told Robert. I overheard them talking about it."

Without taking proper leave of Lady Victoria, Darcy was gone directly.

Darcy was sitting in his study when his cousin Colonel Richard Fitzwilliam strolled into the room in response to his summons.

"Even though I dropped everything to see you, thinking this had to do with Victoria, I do not know that I liked being called away from more pleasurable pursuits merely for the purpose of accommodating your wishes, Darcy."

"Surely you do not suppose I asked you here to discuss your sister. It is just as I expected. She was never with child, and why she would pretend otherwise is beyond comprehension."

"You cannot be surprised. Did I not tell you that my sister was in love with you last year when we were in Kent? I'm only sorry that she went to such lengths to try to entrap you into marriage."

"If only I had listened to you, Victoria's scheme might not have cost me the love of the one woman who means more to me than anyone else in the world."

"When I spoke to my sister before coming to see you, she was going on about Miss Elizabeth Bennet and how she had won. Hence, I surmise you must be speaking of her. However, I'm surprised to hear you speak of losing her in such terms of regret in light of all that has happened."

"What do you mean? Has something happened that I ought to know about?"

"Surely you have heard of the scandal surrounding the youngest Bennet daughter."

"I am afraid I have not. Although your sister implied something appalling has taken place. Indeed, that is the reason I wanted to see you. Victoria said she overheard you and Robert talking."

"I am afraid the news is appalling. The youngest Bennet daughter, you see, has run off. She has thrown herself into George Wickham's power. Rumor has it that the foolish young girl thought he was taking her to Gretna Green, but you and I know him too well to suppose anything of the sort."

"How do you know any of this?"

"It's a consequence of the circles in which I travel."

"Do you know what has been done to recover her?"

"I have heard that the girl's father and her uncle are doing all they can. By all accounts, nothing has been seen or heard of Wickham and the girl since they left Brighton. They most certainly did not travel to Gretna Green. No, if I know anything at all about that vile George Wickham it is that he is buried somewhere in London's underbelly, hiding from the girl's relations as well as a slew of creditors."

Extraordinary Application

There was a flurry of activity at Dunsmore House in preparation for the next day's wedding celebration.

Just the day before, Elizabeth and Lady Sophia had attended another wedding ceremony — one that was rather quiet and low-key, for it was the marriage of her youngest sister, Lydia, to George Wickham. It was a shock to them all, but the wayward couple mysteriously surfaced from whatever hellhole they had been held up in – no doubt one of London's seedier sides – proclaiming their intention to marry. Other than Lady Sophia, Elizabeth, Mr. and Mrs. Gardiner, the officiant and the couple themselves, there were no other guests. Even Mr. and Mrs. Bennet and Elizabeth's other sisters had not been informed. It was a strange affair indeed. The good news was that the Bennet family's reputation would be salvaged in time, and for that Elizabeth was exceedingly grateful.

The last thing Lady Sophia and Elizabeth expected was that one of the people among those coming and going that day would be Lady Catherine de Bourgh. Neither of the former two could think of a probable motive for the latter's coming. Elizabeth had only met Lady Catherine once before and that was during the start of the Season. Elizabeth recalled that her ladyship had been most disagreeable.

Having entered the room with an ungracious air hardly befitting a guest in the home of a duke, Lady Catherine refused all the usual courtesies and asserted her purpose in coming was to speak to Elizabeth in privacy. Assured that Elizabeth's courage would rise in the wake of any challenge put forth by the bad-tempered guest, Lady Sophia quit the room.

"You ought to know, young lady, that I have just heard a report of a most alarming nature that has to do with you and my nephew. I have come here from my brother's home – the Earl of Matlock – and I cannot begin to express my disgust. I went there for the express purpose of putting an end to my niece's lies about Darcy being the father of her unborn child only to learn that she was never with child from the start."

What? Did I rightly hear her ladyship correctly? Did she say that her niece was never with child? This confirms Mr. Darcy's original conjecture that his cousin was lying.

Elizabeth responded to her ladyship with unaffected astonishment. "This information seems to be of a rather personal nature between Mr. Darcy and his cousin. I fail to see what any of this has to do with me."

"I will not be trifled with, young woman. My niece had the audacity to tell me that the favorite wish of two sisters is still not to be realized owing to my nephew's belief that he is in love with you. That young woman has proved herself to be a most egregious liar, and I suspect that what she claims about my nephew's supposed feelings for you is just another instance. Her wild imagination does not end there. She claims that my nephew exercised extraordinary measures to bring about the recovery of your youngest sister from her despicable plight – a young woman of barely sixteen fornicating with a man nearly twice her senior – and that his sole purpose in doing so was to regain your good opinion. She also said that my nephew has long intended to make you an offer of marriage and that he likely has already done so."

"If you believe your niece to be untruthful, what can be your purpose in coming to see me?"

"I determined to come here and have you declare that there is no foundation for her assertions."

"I do not pretend to be obligated to speak on such matters."

"This is not to be borne, Miss Bennet. I insist upon being satisfied. Has my nephew made you an offer of marriage?"

"Again, your ladyship, you may choose to ask me questions of such a personal nature, but I am not obliged to answer."

"You insolent girl! Do you suppose for one instant that I would quietly stand by and allow such a travesty to unfold? If I was not content to allow Darcy to be taken in by my niece – my own flesh and blood – then why would I allow the likes of you to dissuade him?

"From their infancy, my nephew and my daughter, Anne, have been intended for each other. It was the favorite wish of his mother, as well as my own. While they lay in their cradles we planned the union. Now when the wishes of both sisters would be accomplished by their marriage, it is to be threatened by a young woman of inferior birth."

Her ladyship glared at Elizabeth. "Make no mistake—no scandalous twist of fate can alter your inferior bloodline despite your noble connections."

"You fail to take into account that Mr. Darcy and I are wholly equal despite the *scandalous* twist of fate that you expound upon. He is a gentleman and I am a gentleman's daughter!"

"True. You are a gentleman's daughter. But what of your mother? Who are your uncles and aunts? Do not imagine me ignorant of their condition."

"Whatever my connections may be," said Elizabeth, "if your nephew does not object to them, they can be nothing to you."

"I have suffered enough of your impertinence! Tell me once and for all, are you engaged to him?"

Though Elizabeth would not have answered this question merely for the sake of obliging Lady Catherine, she could not but say, after a moment's deliberation, that she was not engaged to the woman's nephew.

Lady Catherine seemed pleased. "And will you promise me never to enter into such an engagement?"

"I will make no promise of the kind."

"Miss Bennet, I am shocked and astonished. I had expected to find you a more reasonable young woman. However, do not deceive yourself into a belief that I will ever recede. I shall not go away until you have given me the assurance I require."

"And I certainly never shall give it. I am not to be intimidated into anything so wholly unreasonable. It is no great secret that you want Mr. Darcy to marry your daughter, but would my giving you the wished-for promise make their marriage any more probable?

"Even if he were attached to me, would my refusing to accept his hand make him wish to bestow it on his cousin? Allow me to say, Lady Catherine, that the arguments with which you have supported this extraordinary application have been as frivolous as the application was ill-judged. You have widely mistaken my character if you think I can be worked on by such persuasions as these. How far your nephew might approve of your interference in his affairs I cannot tell, but you have certainly no right to concern yourself in mine. I must beg, therefore, to be importuned no longer on the subject."

"And this is your real opinion! This is your final resolve! Very well. I shall now know how to act. Do not imagine, Miss Bennet, that your ambition will ever be gratified. I came to try you. I hoped to find you reasonable, but, depend upon it, I will carry my point."

In this manner, Lady Catherine babbled on until she was at the door. Then, turning hastily around, she added, "I take no leave of you, Miss Bennet. I send no compliments to Lady Sophia or His Grace. You deserve no such attention. I am most seriously displeased."

Darcy slowly traced his thumb along the rim of his glass. What a distasteful business it had been — recovering Elizabeth's youngest sister from the scandal she had thrust upon herself as well as her family. Even if Elizabeth were never to learn of his part in arranging the expeditious marriage between Wickham and her youngest sister, it still would have been worth it as recompense for the pain he himself had caused her.

Sitting across the table from Avery at White's, he said, "I understand that congratulations are in order. I wish you and Miss Hamilton all the happiness in the world."

"Thank you, Darcy. As much as I would wish to have you there, I do not think it will be wise in light of the circumstances."

"You are aware, or perhaps you're not by your attitude, but my cousin's accusations against me have proved false, just as I said they would. There is no longer an expectation of our being married."

"I am very happy for you, Darcy; however, I am not sure that changes anything as far as my sister is concerned."

"That is fair enough. However, you ought to know that my feelings for Elizabeth have not changed. Although she refuses to see me, I have not given up on the hope of a future between us."

"You wounded her deeply. Why would she wish to see you?"

"Avery, you know under normal circumstances I would never impose upon our friendship. In such a case as this, it cannot be helped."

"What do you want from me, Darcy?"

"If I could but see her…"

"Darcy, I am not insensitive to your plight as regards my sister, nor have I forgotten what a great friend you have been to my family." Here, Avery paused for a moment. Arising from his chair, he extended his hand to his friend. "You are welcome to be a part of my wedding celebration."

Chapter 28

Words of Approbation

What a grand affair Avery's wedding breakfast was. It was everything that a member of the realm's nuptials ought to be. Everyone praised the duke's new wife, whose elegance and grace were in every way suitable to her elevated rank. Her exquisite gown gave Elizabeth and Lady Sophia to know its procurement alone had to have been the work of many weeks, if not months.

Avery was happy with his choice of bride. Nothing else really mattered, and, regardless of the young woman's humble origins, she was now the

Duchess of Dunsmore. Not only did she have Elizabeth's and Lady Sophia's respect, but she also had their loyalty and support.

However, Elizabeth did have cause to take umbrage with His Grace. He had not said a word to her about Mr. Darcy's being invited to the wedding. She had seen the gentleman earlier that week and had managed successfully to avoid him. That was before her encounter with his aunt, Lady Catherine de Bourgh. Now she wanted to see him. Better stated, she needed to see him. Lady Catherine's tirade had raised more questions than answers, and it had also inspired in Elizabeth a glimmer of hope.

Supposing what she had to say about his involvement in my sister's recovery is true, the very least I can do is thank him on behalf of my family.

When he could, Darcy headed straight towards her. Bowing, he said, "Miss Elizabeth."

She curtsied. "Mr. Darcy."

"It is a pleasure to see you."

"I would say the same, sir. However, I would much rather not say anything here. At the risk of being untoward, pray you will meet me in the library."

His charming smile confirmed he was more than happy to oblige her request. This was indeed a cause for hope.

Alone in the library, Darcy and Elizabeth spoke of many things: his aunt's visit, his cousin's duplicity, her sister's scandal, and Elizabeth's feelings of having failed her family. She had thought she could make a difference in her family's life. Her good intentions had not been enough to protect her sister.

"It was right that you tried to do your best by your family and give your sisters good examples to follow. You must not blame yourself for what happened."

"Yet you went out of your way in saving my sister from ruin. You salvaged my family's reputation and at considerable expense to yourself, I suspect. Let me thank you again and again, in the name of all my family, for the generous compassion that induced you to take so much trouble, and bear so many mortifications, for the sake of discovering Lydia and Mr. Wickham."

"If you will thank me," he replied, "let it be for yourself alone. Your family owe me nothing. As much as I respect them, in coming to your sister's aid as I did, I believe I thought only of you."

"I contend that I am deeply obligated to you, sir. What's more, I might not have learned any of this as soon as I did if it had not been for Lady Catherine."

"No doubt she was most unpleasant. I am sorry."

"Please do not be. Her visit cast a different light on other matters as well."

"How so?"

"Your aunt told me your cousin fabricated the entire scheme from the start, just as you suspected. You, sir, know me well enough to know that I am a very curious creature. Surely there's more to the story."

"My cousin admitted to taking advantage of me, even violating my privacy in a most egregious manner, but she also admitted that nothing of a physical nature occurred between us, despite the impropriety."

"If you are saying what I suspect, it is horrible all the same. She is someone whom you've always admired. You loved her and now you must hate her."

"No — I have too many fond memories of her to ever say that I hate her. Although I feel strongly it will be many years before I truly forgive her. I do not suppose I will ever learn to trust her again."

"Because of that trust, you acted the only way you could. I cannot fault you for that. I might even go as far as to credit you with being honorable for the sacrifice you were prepared to make on your cousin's behalf."

"I am sure there are many who would beg to differ."

"Let others say what they will. You and I know better."

"Still, I feel as though I ought to make amends to you for the disappointment you suffered."

"Now it is my turn to say you owe me nothing. I might spend the rest of my life trying to repay you for all you have done for me and my family and all my efforts would prove insufficient."

"I would much rather prefer you make better use of your time simply sharing my love." Darcy took her by the hand. "Elizabeth, it goes without saying that I'm sorry to have wounded you. I always suspected my cousin was lying. Now that we know the truth, tell me it is not too late. Pray tell me we can rid ourselves of the memory of this most harrowing few months and start anew. Dare I ask too much that this day might be the first day of the rest of our lives together?"

"Sir, do you not suppose that such an act as you propose might seem a bit rash?"

"Indeed I do not. How I wish I had offered you my hand before you left Pemberley. I love you – most ardently – and I do not intend to let another day go by without proving it to you. I would like to start this very moment by asking you if you would do me the honor of accepting my hand."

As he was holding her hand, Elizabeth felt

compelled to brush a kiss across his knuckles. "Sir, nothing would give me more pleasure."

"Truly—you mean to say this is finally happening? No more waiting?"

"I would say that you and I have waited long enough."

Moistening his lips, Darcy leaned forward. As they closed their eyes, their lips met. How she had missed the soft feel of his lips on hers. She missed the sweet taste and his gentle coaxing, urging her to surrender her inhibitions and enjoy all that a kiss from the man whom she loved occasioned.

At length, the sound of someone clearing his throat commanded their attention and thus drew them apart. "This had better mean what I hope it means."

Biting her lower lip and hence relishing the lingering taste of her lover's, she looked at the unexpected third party rather sheepishly. The three of them could not help but smile. In such a case as this, what better words of approbation from an older brother might Elizabeth hope for?

A Tender Moment

A very's insistence that Elizabeth's companion,
Miss Greene, accompany her in Mr. Darcy's carriage on her return trip to Hertfordshire vexed Elizabeth exceedingly. True, decorum dictated that a single
woman not travel alone with a single gentleman.
However, it was not as though she and Darcy had not
bent their fair share of rules over the past several days
since their betrothal. With both of them vowing that
they never wished to be parted again, it was all they
could do to stay away from each other. Be it early
morning strolls in the park, middays spent reading in

the library, or dinner parties at either Dunsmore House or Darcy's townhouse, Elizabeth and Darcy were nearly inseparable.

Thus, when Mr. Darcy asked Elizabeth to contrive to sit opposite her faithful companion in order that he might sit next to her, she willingly obliged.

Elizabeth supposed she had the steady lull of the carriage combined with the bright sun peeping through the windows to thank for Miss Greene's persistent yawns and occasional nods. Oh, how she wished the other woman would simply succumb to slumber's beckoning call rather than continue fighting it.

Elizabeth was gazing out the window thinking of the promising prospects that awaited her once she and Mr. Darcy were married when she felt a light brush against her hand. Moments later, she felt a gentle squeeze. She closed her eyes and relished the frissons of pleasure coaxing all over her body. In a flash, she opened them and threw a furtive glance in Miss Greene's direction only to find that her wish had come true. Next, she glimpsed her betrothed. The smoldering look in his eyes told her that he likely had been wishing the same thing.

He raised her hand to his lips and brushed a kiss across her knuckles. As much as Darcy did not like the added scrutiny that his friend had subjected him to of late as it regarded Elizabeth, he could not fault Avery, especially given his body's reaction to her whenever they were this close. No doubt, were his own sister, Georgiana, engaged to a man so evidently and so violently in love with her, Darcy would exercise the same guarded measures as His Grace.

All he could think about from the moment Elizabeth had agreed to be his wife was how long it would be before the blessed event took place. Fortunately, it would not be very long at all. As much as Elizabeth may have wished for a lengthy stay in Hertfordshire, she dearly wanted Avery to be there on her special day, which dictated he delay his extended wedding journey. Assured his petition for Elizabeth's hand would be met with Mr. Bennet's approval, Darcy had even procured a special license. *Soon Elizabeth will be all mine.*

Releasing her hand, Darcy casually outstretched his arm and then rested it along the back of the seat. He claimed her hand once more with his free hand, allowing his fingers to brush over her skin. Slowly, he leaned in until his lips were within inches of hers.

"Sir," she said, her voice barely above a whisper, her breath warm, her amazing dark eyes questioning.

Her lips were moist, slightly parted and inviting and he wanted nothing more than to kiss her. He leaned even closer and then whispered in her ear. "I was beginning to think she would never fall asleep."

The steady rise and fall of her chest surely evidenced the arousing effect this man had on all her sensibilities. She swallowed. "You, sir, are incorrigible."

At length, Darcy's arm fell from the back of the seat and rested behind Elizabeth's body, his fingers about her waist. His lingering touch set every inch of her being tingling inside.

She settled herself a little closer, laid her head on his chest, and the two clasped opposite hands — their fingers intertwined. Closing her eyes, Elizabeth reminded herself to breathe. She had not a single care that Miss Greene might awaken. Enjoying a tender moment like this with the man who had long ago captured her heart was something she would not have traded for anything in the world.

Soon after Darcy and Elizabeth arrived at Longbourn, he requested a private audience with Mr. Bennet, and the two of them withdrew to the library. This gave rise to a modicum of agitation on Elizabeth's part. Not that she feared her father's opposition, but she did not like the idea of his being made unhappy over her approaching removal to Derbyshire.

Mr. Darcy's absence did not immediately concern Mrs. Bennet, and, for that, Elizabeth was grateful for it allowed her time to converse intimately with her dearest Jane.

Speaking softly, Jane said, "First, Mr. Darcy escorted you to Longbourn from London, and then he immediately sought a private audience with Papa. Pray tell me this means exactly what I think it means, dearest Lizzy."

Elizabeth could not hide her joy. "Indeed, Jane, I am the happiest creature in the world. Perhaps other people have said so before, but not one with such justification, I am sure."

"It is just as I always knew it would be. I contend that you and Mr. Darcy were fashioned for each other. I do not know that I have ever seen you as happy as you are when he and you are in mutual accord."

"Indeed. There was a time when we were all together in London when I was given to believe that this moment would never come."

"Oh, Lizzy, let us not dwell on misery when we had much better embrace your philosophy to think only of the past as its remembrance gives you pleasure."

Jane would receive no argument from Elizabeth on that score and soon they began to talk about the events of the past few days leading to that particular moment. When Mr. Darcy appeared again, Elizabeth, a little relieved by his smile, took Jane's hand and gave it a gentle squeeze. In a few minutes, he approached the table where she and Jane sat. "Go to your father," he said in a voice barely above a whisper. "He waits for you in the library." She was gone directly.

Mr. Bennet was standing at the window, looking out at the garden when Elizabeth entered the room.

"Mr. Darcy said you wished to speak with me, Papa."

"Yes, come closer, my dear Lizzy," said her father, turning to greet her. "I have given him my consent. He is the kind of man, indeed, to whom I should never dare refuse anything for which he condescended to ask. I now give it to you, although I contend that no one can be truly worthy of you. Nevertheless, if I have to part with you, it ought to be with him. You will pardon my saying this, but I had hoped this day would have come much later. To own the truth, the instant I watched you step down from the carriage the past autumn, I knew our time with you was not meant to last."

"Papa, you speak as though you're losing me, when nothing could be further from the truth."

"In all the ways that matter, I am losing you. Say what you will, but you are a young bride. I imagine your entire focus will be on building a life with your husband, as it ought to be."

"Perhaps you should not think of this as losing a daughter, but rather as gaining a son."

Mr. Bennet spoke of what a fine son-in-law Mr. Darcy would be. To complete her papa's favorable impression, Elizabeth then told him what Mr. Darcy had voluntarily done for Lydia.

Having listened to his daughter with aston-ishment, Mr. Bennet said, "This is a day of wonders, indeed! And so Darcy did everything: made up the match, gave the money, paid the fellow's debts, and got him his commission in the north of England! I had supposed it had been your uncle's doing, in which case I would have insisted on paying him. I suppose I ought to extend the same consideration to your Mr. Darcy."

She held up her hand. "No, Papa. He would not want you to."

"The truth is that, even if I lived on for another two hundred years, I scarcely doubt I would ever be able to truly repay him for all he has done on behalf of our family, but in this case I think I shall offer to pay him all the same. No doubt he will rant and storm about his love for you, and that will be an end of the matter."

"Oh, Papa," cried Elizabeth lovingly. She

threw her arms around him. "I shall miss you exceedingly. Promise me you will come to Pemberley."

"I shall ponder the matter, my Lizzy."

"Indeed you must and should you need any greater inducement than your affection for me, I beg you to take into account that the library at Pemberley, being the work of many generations, is splendid."

Chapter 30

Incandescently Happy

Happy for all their maternal feelings was the day on which both Mrs. Bennet and Lady Sophia Montlake watched Elizabeth and Mr. Darcy exchange wedding vows.

Her ladyship could rightfully say that she always knew it would be this way. She had known even before Elizabeth did that the latter was destined to marry the handsome Mr. Darcy. But, then again, she supposed, a mother always has a way of knowing such things.

Avery had been overjoyed to delay his honeymoon journey for the sake of seeing his sister and one of his closest friends united in matrimony. To Elizabeth's surprise, Avery was quite happy to play the role of the dutiful, protective older brother, and he insisted that Mr. Bennet do the honors of negotiating Elizabeth's marriage settlement. Her fifty thousand pound dowry aside, Avery contended that the older gentleman was her father after all, a status that trumped everything, even the prerogative of a duke.

Although Elizabeth and Miss Darcy had spent little time together during the past, they would soon make up for it. Indeed, Darcy and Elizabeth decided that Georgiana would be removed from her London establishment to reside with them at Pemberley. Having grown accustomed to the idea of having sisters, Elizabeth liked this scheme very much.

As for Darcy's other relatives, Lord Matlock did indeed send his daughter away, but not to Bedlam as he had suggested. He surmised she was cunning and clever, not stark raving mad. A year in Scotland with her mother's distant relations was to be her penance.

Lady Catherine was extremely indignant over the marriage of her nephew. Giving way to all the genuine frankness of her character, of which she so often boasted, she replied as one might have expected to the letter Darcy sent announcing his engagement. Her language was so very abusive, especially of Elizabeth and her relatives, and she decried with equal venom the degradation of the shades of Pemberley being thus polluted, that he pronounced her ladyship would be considered a stranger to him.

Being ever the loyal friend, Bingley returned to Netherfield for the wedding, which was indeed a very good thing. His declaration that he planned to stay for the remainder of the year was truly a cause for joy. Moreover, in spite of Jane's insistence that she and the gentleman were no more than indifferent acquaintances, her mother's renewed hopes and effusive affirmations that her eldest daughter was to be the next mistress of Netherfield did not meet with Jane's displeasure.

Later that day, when all the wedding breakfast guests were gone, Mrs. Bennet said to her husband, "Two daughters married and with hardly any trouble to myself. I do not need to tell you how much easier this makes the rest of my job. Soon I shall have nothing left to wish for."

"How do you suppose that, my dear?"

"Why, surely you know that Lizzy's marriage alone shall put the other girls in the path of many rich gentlemen. It is already happening to our Jane as it has been the means of Mr. Bingley's return. I have it on good authority that he means to do right by her this time. Oh, what a happy day this is!"

Dunsmore Estate, some weeks later

How different it was walking along the pristine lane leading to the Dunsmore burial place now than when she first went that way during that mournful day when the former Duke of Dunsmore was laid to rest. The feelings she now suffered were in no way akin to those she had felt then. The last time she had traveled that path, she felt sorrow, pain, and loss. Now she did not know exactly how she felt. All Elizabeth knew was that she needed to be there.

When she arrived at His Grace's tomb, she was silent and reverent. At length she spoke. "I came here to tell you that I do not hate you, Your Grace. Nor do I forgive you." Elizabeth swallowed back her tears. "From the moment you abducted me from the streets of Lambton and in so doing forever altered the course of my life until the day I sat by your bedside and watched you take your final breath, I never knew you at all. You were a stranger to me." Here, she paused again for a bit of quiet reflection.

"More than once, of late, I have been reminded of my own philosophy to think only of the past as its remembrance brings me pleasure. As I can think of no more fitting occasion to embrace that sentiment, I must hereby vow to think of you no more."

Elizabeth exhaled deeply when she came from the cemetery and saw Darcy standing there by the gate waiting for her. Each closing the distance between them, they soon stood face-to-face.

Darcy rested his forehead against hers. "Are you ready to leave, my love?"

"I am indeed. Please take me home ... to Pemberley."

He kissed her and then they joined hands. Walking hand in hand with her husband, Elizabeth was overcome with a sense of knowing. With him was where she belonged. Forever more there would be no doubt as to who she was. Not Lady Elizabeth Montlake. Not Miss Elizabeth Bennet.

I am Mrs. Elizabeth Darcy, the mistress of Pemberley and the incandescently happy wife of Mr. Fitzwilliam Darcy, whom I shall forever regard as the best man in the world.

Author

P. O. Dixon is a writer as well as an entertainer. Historical England and its days of yore fascinate her. She, in particular, loves the Regency period with its strict mores and oh so proper decorum. Her ardent appreciation of Jane Austen's timeless works set her on the writer's journey.

Visit podixon.com and find out more about Dixon's writings.

.

Author's Books

§ A Darcy and Elizabeth Love Affair Series:

A Lasting Love Affair: Darcy and Elizabeth (Book 1)
'Tis the Season for Matchmaking: A Lasting Love Affair
Continues (Book 2)

§ Pride and Prejudice Untold Series:

To Have His Cake (and Eat It Too): Mr. Darcy's Tale (Book 1)
What He Would Not Do: Mr. Darcy's Tale Continues (Book 2)
Lady Harriette: Fitzwilliam's Heart and Soul (Book 3)

§ Darcy and Elizabeth Short Stories Series (Stand-alone Books):

Pride and Sensuality (Book 1)
Expecting His Proposal (Book 2)
A Tender Moment (Book 3)

§ Darcy and the Young Knight's Quest Series:

He Taught Me to Hope (Book 1)
The Mission: He Taught Me to Hope Christmas Vignette (Book 2)
Hope and Sensibility (Book 3)

§ Pride and Prejudice Everything Will Change Series:

Lady Elizabeth (Book 1)
So Far Away (Book 2)

§ Pride and Prejudice Variations Collection Series (Stand-alone Books):

Almost Persuaded: Miss Mary King
Bewitched, Body and Soul: Miss Elizabeth Bennet
Love Will Grow: A Pride and Prejudice Story
Still a Young Man: Darcy Is In Love
Only a Heartbeat Away: Pride and Prejudice Novella
Matter of Trust: The Shades of Pemberley

Made in the USA
Middletown, DE
14 August 2015